MW01243102

DAVE DAWSON ON THE RUSSIAN FRONT

BY Robert Sidney Bowen

Dave Dawson on the Russian Front

BY Robert Sidney Bowen

ISBN 1519556942
EAN-13   978-1519556943

Published by Alacrity Press, 2016
All rights reserved.
www.alacritypress.com

This book is a product of its time. Some of the terms and views expressed by the author may reflect common values and usage of his day that are contrary to modern values. They should be viewed in that context.

ALACRITY
PRESS

Contents

Russian soldiers fire a machine gun during the Battle of Kursk.

CHAPTER ONE
MYSTERY MAN

"Okay, okay!" Dave Dawson growled, and rolled over to a more comfortable position in the hotel bed. "It's dear old England. A wonderful country, a great place. And you're tickled silly to be here. Okay, I agree with every word you say. God save the King, and there'll always be an England. *Now*, will you let a guy get some sleep?"

"But you don't understand what it means to me, Dave." Freddy Farmer spoke through the darkness from the other bed. "This is my native land, my home, and I've—"

"Gone completely screwy!" Dawson snapped. "Sweet tripe! You were here only two days ago. Two days you've been away, and you're sounding off as though you'd been away for a million years. Just a two day jaunt over to France, and the guy starts flag waving. My pal, much as I like you, you are a pain in seventeen different places at the same time. Go to sleep, you bow-legged Commando!"[1]

"Just what I've said quite often," Freddy said placidly. "It takes an Englishman to really appreciate his homeland. Two years or two days, what does it matter? The joy that is his upon arriving back home is always the same. Do you see what I mean, Dave?"

Dawson groaned, sat up in bed, and switched on the table lamp. But as he did so he took a quick automatic glance at the room windows to make sure that the blackout curtains were drawn and securely fastened. Then he hunched around in bed and glared at his closest and dearest friend in the world.

"The day will come!" he snarled. "So help me, the day will come!"

The English-born air ace blinked, and looked blank.

"Eh?" he echoed. "What say, Dave?"

"Just that the day will come, so help me!" Dawson answered, and leveled a stiff forefinger. "The day will come when I'll forget I like you, and will up and bust you right on your snoot. For cat's sake, Freddy! You're worse than a woman, from what I hear of them. Don't you ever shut up?"

Freddy Farmer propped a hand under his head and grinned.

"But I don't feel sleepy," he said. "I want to talk. Don't you? Now, really, you're not sleepy, are you, Dave? After all, we haven't had much time to talk since we got back from that Commando show in Occupied France. We've—I say! What's the matter, old fellow?"

---

1. *Dave Dawson With the Commandos.*

The last was because Dawson's hands had come up in an attitude of prayer, and his lips were moving soundlessly.

"Just calling for strength," he told his pal. "For a second there I almost wished that you had been left behind, you doggone phonograph record. Look, pal, see these lines on my face? And these pouches under my eyes? Well, that's not from age. Just because I'm tired."

Freddy Farmer stared hard, and his face flooded with sympathy. However, there was a very wicked gleam in his eyes.

"I say, Dave, old thing!" he murmured. "I'm frightfully sorry, no end. I thought—well, as you Yanks say, that you could take it. I didn't dream that little Commando show in Occupied France would do you in so much. Put out the light, you poor fellow, and try to get some sleep. Want me to send down to the chemist shop for something to make you sleep? Drugstore, you call it in the States, don't you?"

Dawson carefully settled himself in a sitting position, and then, clasping his hands in his lap, he started to count.

"One—two—three—four—five—!"

"I say, Dave, what's up?" Freddy Farmer cried in alarm.

"When I get to ten, you'll find out!" Dawson barked. Then, with a heavy sigh, "Okay, okay, you want to talk, so what chance have I got? I couldn't sleep, now, if I were hit by a truck. But just one thing, Freddy Farmer: keep this night in your memory, always!"

"Why, Dave?"

"Just never mind, sweetheart!" Dave grunted. "Skip it for the present. As you were saying?"

"Oh, so you want to talk, old thing?" the English youth echoed, and grinned maliciously. "Splendid! It is nice to be back in England, isn't it?"

"I could answer that, but my folks brought me up to act like a gentleman!" Dawson snapped. "What else, Edison?"

"Edison?"

"The inventor of the phonograph," Dawson said. "Turn the record and put in a new needle!"

"Well, I was wondering—" the English youth murmured, as he let the wisecrack sail right over his head—"I was wondering what next, Dave?"

"More loss of sleep," Dawson flung at him, "because of more useless talk at three in the morning from a certain nit-wit. And, I do mean you!"

"And the same to you, sir!" Freddy came right back at him, and made a face. "But I am still wondering what's going to happen next?"

"Who cares, so long at it's action against those dirty Nazis," Dawson said.

"Quite!" the English youth murmured. "But you're a very tired little fellow. Go on back to sleep. I'll tell you about it in the morning. That'll be time enough. Good night, Dave. Or rather, good morning."

Freddy reached a hand toward the table lamp between the twin beds, but Dave grabbed hold of it in time.

"Nix!" he said. "That look on your face makes me suspicious, young fellow. You've got something important on your mind. I can tell. Come on, now. Let's have it, pal."

"Oh, I fancy it will keep until morning," Freddy Farmer said with a wicked grin. "Go get your beauty sleep. After all, it arrived after you had gone to sleep. So what's the difference?"

By now Dawson was wide awake, and as he swung his legs out from under the covers there was a dangerous glint in his eyes.

"Stop right there, pal!" he grunted, and leveled a finger. "What came after I'd gone to sleep? Do you tell me, or do I toss you through that window, blackout curtains and all?"

"Oh no you don't!" the English youth cried as he leaped out of bed on the far side. "Calm down, young fellow, and I'll tell you. Stay put, or not a word will I tell you!"

Dawson relaxed and sank back on his bed.

"Okay, but it had better be good!" he growled through a yawn. "Okay, what's the big mystery?"

"It was a phone call," Freddy Farmer said with a jerk of his head toward the instrument on the wall. "From the Air Ministry. We are to report at Room Twelve Hundred at eight o'clock in the morning."

"Hey, they can't do that to us!" Dave cried. "We're supposed to be on leave. We—Did the chap at the other end say what it was all about?"

Freddy Farmer shook his head and slid back into bed.

"Not a word," he said. "Naturally, I asked questions. But that's all the good it did me. The chap was very brusque. Report at eight, and that's that."

Dawson sighed and gave a sad shake of his head.

"Not that I don't want to do my part in trimming the Nazis," he said, "but, my gosh, I could do with at least a couple of days leave. Why, I haven't even had time to see a movie in months. Oh, well, maybe it's for something unimportant."

"I doubt it," Freddy Farmer said emphatically. "I guess you've forgotten Room Twelve Hundred at the Air Ministry, Dave."

"Huh?" Dawson echoed, jerking his head up. "Room—? Holy smoke! That's Royal Air Force Intelligence! But it doesn't make sense, Freddy. We're not in the R.A.F. now. We're with the Yank forces!"

"Quite!" the English-born air ace grunted. "But I fancy Air Ministry wouldn't have phoned that order if they hadn't first obtained permission of Yank G.H.Q. But what difference does it make, anyway, if it's Yank G.H.Q. or the Air Ministry? Either of them could detail a job to us. But the important thing to me is, what is it this time?"

"The fellow on the phone didn't give you any kind of a hint?" Dawson persisted.

The English youth shook his head.

"Not the faintest," he replied. "We'll just have to wait and find out, I'm afraid."

Dawson groaned and glanced at the clock on the night table. The hands showed him it was exactly sixteen minutes to four. Just four hours and sixteen minutes to wait!

"Nuts!" he sighed, and slid down under the covers. "I wish I hadn't made you tell me, pal. Now there's a fat chance that I'll get any more sleep! You don't happen to have a deck of cards around, do you? We could kill time with some two-handed rummy."

"Sorry," Freddy Farmer said. "Not a card. But I'll sing to you, if you like."

"Never!" Dawson cried out in mock protest. "Spare me that, please, sir. Besides, I don't want to have the authorities piling in here to arrest you for impersonating the air raid sirens. Nix! I'll permit you to sing over my dead body. I'll—Oh, darn it! What do you suppose they've got cooked up for us in Room Twelve Hundred at the Air Ministry?"

"How I wish I knew!" Freddy Farmer breathed solemnly. "But if past experience means anything, there's one thing we can bank on, no doubt."

"Which would be?" Dawson grunted.

"A messy job of some kind," the English youth opined. "They seem to save that sort of thing especially for us."

"Check and double check!" Dawson murmured. "You've got something there, pal. And how!"

And with that both boys lapsed into silence, and stared thoughtful and scowlingly up at the hotel room ceiling.

CHAPTER TWO
ROOM 1200

Any period of time will pass if you'll just wait long enough, and so eventually it was eight o'clock in the morning, and the two air aces had paused before Room Twelve Hundred at the Air Ministry. They had paused by unspoken mutual consent. And now as their eyes met they both grinned, and lifted their right hands with the middle fingers crossed over the indexes.

"Here's for luck, or something," Dave Dawson murmured with a wink.

"Quite," Freddy Farmer echoed. "At least, I hope it won't be *bad* luck."

For a couple of seconds more the two youths hesitated, and then Dave Dawson took a deep breath, turned the door knob, and pushed the door open. He entered the small outer office with Freddy Farmer right at his heels. A Flight Lieutenant seated at the small desk took one swift look at their American Air Force uniforms and recognized them at once.

"Good morning, Captains," he said with a smile. "I'll tell Air Vice-Marshal Leman, and Colonel Welsh, that you are here."

Both Dave and Freddy instantly stiffened and went wide-eyed. It was Dawson who found his tongue first.

"What's that, Flight Lieutenant?" he got out. "Did I hear you say Colonel Welsh? You don't mean Colonel Welsh, chief of the U.S. Armed Forces Intelligence?"

"That's exactly who I mean," the Flight Lieutenant replied. "He arrived in England by bomber yesterday. Just a moment, please, and I'll let them know you're here."

The Flight Lieutenant went over to a huge solid oak door, knocked on it, and then stepped through and closed it behind him. Dave and Freddy chose that moment to gape puzzle-eyed at each other.

"Well, what do you know!" Dawson finally breathed. "Colonel Welsh, who had us hauled out of the R.A.F. in the first place!"[2]

"I know," the English youth echoed. "Fancy, meeting him here in London. Well, I guess that certainly means that something new has been cooked up for us. Good grief! His name was the farthest from my mind!"

"You and me both!" Dawson said with a nod. "And it sure does mean that plenty's on the fire, if Colonel Welsh is over here. But it'll be good to meet him again. He always rated tops with me."

"Quite!" the English youth murmured.

---

2. *Dave Dawson With The Pacific Fleet.*

And that's as far as he got. At that moment the Flight Lieutenant opened the huge solid oak door, and motioned for them to come into the inner office. They did, with Dawson leading the way, and so it was his hand that was grasped first by the thin-faced officer in the uniform of a U.S. Infantry Colonel.

"Well, Dawson, I'm certainly mighty glad to meet you again!" the Colonel greeted him. "And you, too, Farmer. Neither of you has changed a bit."

"Thank you, sir," Dawson smiled back at him. "And it's good to meet you again. This is certainly one big surprise."

"Quite, sir," Freddy echoed as he, too, shook hands with the Colonel. "I hope you had a nice flight across."

"A perfect hop," the senior officer said. "But I'm forgetting my manners. Air Vice-Marshal Leman, let me present Captains Dawson and Farmer. But perhaps you've already met?"

The good looking Air Force officer, who had sat smiling behind a desk that seemed to fill half the room, got up instantly and came around it with his hand outstretched.

"No, but I've certainly heard no end of things about you two," he said as he shook hands with both boys. "But who hasn't, for that matter?" he continued with a chuckle. "Including Adolf Hitler, of course. There, have chairs, Gentlemen. I can see it in your faces that you are wondering no end what this is all about. Well, Colonel, I fancy you'd better do the talking for us, eh?"

The senior American officer smiled, nodded, and then waited until everybody was comfortably seated in chairs.

"I've a job for you," he presently told the two youths bluntly. "And I want to say right here that it is probably the toughest assignment you ever received. Feel like taking a crack at something *really* tough?"

Dave Dawson leaned forward on the edge of his chair, and nodded eagerly. All thoughts of leave were gone from his brain now. Just the sight of Colonel Welsh had changed everything all around. He was more than ever anxious for action.

"The tougher it is the better I'll like it, sir," he said with a grin. "Speaking for myself, of course."

"Oh, you're jolly well speaking for me, too!" Freddy Farmer spoke up quickly. "Besides, you'd have to have me along to watch out for you, you know."

Everybody chuckled at that remark, and then Colonel Welsh's thin face became very grave and serious.

"I really meant that, just the same," he said with a grim nod. "This one is really tough, and your chances of pulling it off successfully are about one in six million, roughly speaking."

"The odds have been pretty big against us in the past, sir," Dave said quietly. "But where are we heading this time, or shouldn't I ask yet?"

"You may, and I'll answer it," Colonel Welsh replied. "This time it's Russia."

That brought both youths up stiff and straight on the edges of their chairs.

"Russia?" Dave gasped out.

"Russia?" Freddy Farmer echoed incredulously. "Good grief!"

"That's right, Russia," Colonel Welsh repeated. "But just where in Russia, the good Lord Himself alone knows. To be perfectly frank, it's quite possible that I'm sending you after no more than a handful of Russian air. That's why I say the odds against your success are about one in six million. However, if by any possible chance you do pull this one off, why then—"

The American Intelligence Chief paused and made a little gesture with his hands.

"Why then," he continued a moment later, "Civilization will owe you a far bigger debt of gratitude than it does now, even."

Neither of the boys said anything. They just sat quietly, with their eyes fixed on the senior officer, and waited for him to continue. However, when the Colonel spoke again it was not to the boys. He addressed himself to Air Vice-Marshal Leman.

"On second thought, sir," he said, "perhaps you'd better tell your part of it first. Then I'll take it up from there."

The senior R.A.F. officer shrugged and nodded.

"Very well, if you like, Colonel," he said. And then, turning to the two air aces, he began, "This all started back in the summer of 1939, just before Hitler started into Poland. Of course, anybody with half an eye, or half an ear, could have both seen and heard things that would have left no doubt of what the Nazis had up their sleeves. We of Intelligence knew perfectly well that no amount of appeasement would change Hitler's plans one single bit. We knew that the man was no more than a mad dog, and that only a bullet in the brain could stop him. However, the Government in power at the time thought otherwise, and tried to—Well, all that blasted business of the Munich meeting is dead history now. So it doesn't help anything to bring it out into the light again."

The R.A.F. Intelligence chief paused for breath and to clear his throat. Then he made a little gesture with one hand and continued.

"What I'm trying to bring out," he said, "is that though there was hope in certain quarters that something could be done to stop Hitler at that time, and without bloodshed, we of Intelligence were carrying on as though we were actually at war. Or at least on the brink of war, which of course we were. Anyway, our agents were all over Europe gathering every bit of information possible, and making underground contacts that might prove useful when, and if, the guns started firing. Well, one of my agents—and we'll call him Jones for the moment—had a rare bit of luck. It was one of those things that happen say once in a hundred years. It happened as a result of no effort of his part, either. It—well, it was simply a bit of absolutely lucky coincidence.

"This Jones, having completed a small mission in Prague, in Czecho-slovakia, was on his way by train to Krakow, Poland, when right at the borders of Germany, Czechoslovakia, and Poland, the train was wrecked. Split rails caused the wreck, and some sixty odd persons were killed. For-tunately, Jones was in one of the three cars that remained on the track, and he received no more than a severe shaking up. Well, it so happened that a Nazi trade mission on the way to Moscow was aboard the train, and two of its members were killed. That, of course, made it more than just an ordinary train wreck. According to Jones the whole place was alive with Nazi officials in no time at all. Actually the exact location of the wreck was a good mile within the Polish borders, but that didn't bother the Nazis any. They regarded it as German ground and took complete charge of everything at once. The Polish officials objected, but that's all the good it did them. Incidentally, the thing did not appear in the public prints, but as a matter of record that wreck was the first of the so-called border incidents that terminated with the Nazi invasion, and slaughter, of Poland."

Air Vice-Marshal Leman paused again, and sat staring off into space as though choosing the words he would speak next. And when he did speak again there was just the faintest trace of bitter disappointment in his voice.

"Whether the wreck was an accident, or was deliberately planned," he continued, "will never be known. However, the Nazis instantly took it as an act of sabotage and, in true Nazi fashion, started arresting people left and right. They arrested people who were actually on the train, as well as a lot of the male inhabitants of a small village that bordered that stretch of track. And anybody who even so much as offered a single word of protest was immediately clubbed half to death, and definitely regarded by the Nazis as one of the perpetrators of the so called crime against the Third Reich. Well, you can imagine what a madhouse that place was, with passengers dead and dying, others trying to do what they could for the injured, and the Nazi brutes pounding roughshod over everything and everybody. It was indeed a perfect pre-view of what was to come on a much more gigantic scale.

"Well, Jones, being no more than shaken up a bit, joined those who were doing what they could to help the injured. He came upon one man who was pinned under the shattered end of one car. The man was conscious, but he was bleeding at the mouth, and his chest was horribly crushed. Jones took him for a German, but that didn't make any difference at the time. He started trying to get the pieces of the shattered car off the man and drag him free in case fire broke out. It was a pretty hopeless task. The slightest movement made the pinned man's face go grey with pain, and finally he begged Jones—and in perfect English, mind you—just to let him stay where he was. The intense pain of being rescued was too much for him. And no sooner had he spoken the plea than the surprising thing happened. The injured man whispered for Jones to bend close, and listen to what he had to say. Jones did just that, and the man said that he was a Russian by birth but had lived most of his life in Germany. He said that he had discovered a horrible plot to wipe the Soviet Republic from the face of the earth. That he had learned every detail of Hitler's mad plan to conquer and enslave the entire world!"

The R.A.F. officer stopped short and smiled almost apologetically.

"I know what you must be thinking," he said to the two air aces, who sat motionless and just a little bit wide-eyed. "You're thinking that perhaps I've gone a bit balmy, or that I'm reciting a bit from one of those crazy war stories that are being so widely read these days. But that's not true. All this actually *did* happen. In short, over a month before the war actually started, one man pinned under a wrecked railroad train just inside the Polish border knew every detail of Hitler's entire war plan. And what's more, he gave *half* of that invaluable information to the British Intelligence agent I've called Jones!"

CHAPTER THREE
FATE LAUGHS

The echo of Air Vice-Marshal Leman's last words seemed to hang in the air for long seconds. And then suddenly the echo faded out and the room was filled with a silence in which a pin could have been heard to drop. Dave Dawson gulped softly as he let the clamped air from his lungs, and inched forward on the edge of his chair.

"Only half the information, sir?" he questioned. "So it didn't do Agent Jones any good?"

The senior R.A.F. officer smiled sadly, and seemed to emphasize his feelings with a soft sigh.

"Let me continue with the story, and I think your question will be answered, Dawson," he said. "Yes, the injured man gave Jones only half the information he had collected. But even that half didn't help any. You see, this man had written down everything that he had learned. According to Jones he must have done it with a needle point pen, and under a magnifying glass. It filled two sheets of ordinary manuscript paper, on both sides. It was sewn in his coat, and he got Jones to take it out for him. And then the man tore the two sheets in half and gave half to Jones. Then he tore his half to bits, put them in his mouth and swallowed them!"

"Well, for cats' sake!" Dave Dawson blurted out before he could check himself.

"Quite!" the Air Vice-Marshal said with a faint smile. "It was quite a mad thing to do, considering. But we must suppose that the poor chap was probably half mad from the pain he was suffering. And of course, Jones had naturally not revealed his true identity. Well, anyway, this man told Jones to get away from the spot as soon as he could, and reach the village of Tobolsk as soon as he could. Tobolsk doesn't appear on any of the maps, but it is a tiny village situated about eighty miles west of Stalingrad on the Volga. He told Jones to deliver his half of that precious information to a farmer who lived in Tobolsk. And—well, that's where the real hard luck began to set in."

"Beg pardon, sir?" Freddy Farmer murmured as the senior officer suddenly lapsed into silence and sat scowling darkly down at the top of his desk. "You mean, sir, that Agent Jones wasn't able to contact this farmer in Tobolsk?"

"I mean much more than that!" the other replied with a grimace. "I mean that everything simply went from bad to worse. To begin with, Jones was unable to catch the name of the man he was to contact in Tobolsk. He asked the injured man to repeat it, but it wasn't repeated. The man had become unconscious. Jones had no chance to try to revive him, or to wait for the man to regain consciousness either, for at that moment a party of Nazis swept down on him, thrust him to one side and started getting the injured man out from under the wreckage. It seems that they had suddenly decided that the poor devil had had an active part in causing the wreck. I know that sounds incredible. But I ask you, is there anything sane about the Nazi mind, let alone their actions?"

"Not the ones I've run up against," Dawson grunted with a shake of his head.

"Definitely not!" Freddy Farmer agreed. "But what rotten luck for Agent Jones!"

"And only the beginning!" Air Vice-Marshal Leman growled in his throat. "As Jones stood there quite helpless, the Nazis hauled that poor chap out from under the wreckage and whisked him away, just like that. There was absolutely nothing Jones could do about it without getting into trouble himself. After all, he certainly couldn't take any chances of being arrested. Himmler, of course, knew full well that we had our agents all over Europe, and with war just around the corner it would be all up with any of the poor chaps who were caught. War or no war, we'd certainly never hear from them again. And we couldn't very well admit that they were agents of ours and ask the German Government to release them. Once an agent goes out on a mission he is absolutely on his own. If he gets into a tight corner it's up to him to get himself out of it. To assist him would simply tip our hand, and unquestionably disrupt our entire espionage system. And—"

The R.A.F. Intelligence officer stopped short with a little laugh.

"But I'm a fine one to be telling that to you two chaps, who have actually experienced the situation more than once," he said. "Of course you understand what Jones was up against. His hands were tied, and he simply couldn't make any move without walking straight into the clutches of the Nazis. However, his very good judgment didn't gain him a single thing. He *was* arrested by the Nazis!"

"Arrested?" Freddy Farmer gasped. "Good grief! What for?"

"For the same reason other passengers aboard the train were arrested," the Air Vice-Marshal replied. "Simply for no good reason at all, other than the fact that the Nazis figured they weren't functioning according to plan unless they made some arrest. Anyway, Jones was presently arrested along with the others, perhaps because he was seen talking to the injured man. At any rate, they arrested him and herded him into one of the several police vans that had mysteriously appeared out of nowhere. Just picture what must have been going on in his mind! Stuffed down in one of his pockets were two halves of sheet paper containing data on Hitler's war plans for ultimate world conquest. And there he was in a Nazi prison van under guard, and being driven *back into Germany.*"

"Not so good!" Dawson grunted impulsively. "Right behind the old eight ball, and how!"

"Eh?" the R.A.F. Intelligence chief echoed with arched eyebrows.

"An American expression, sir," Colonel Welsh spoke up with a chuckle. "Dawson means that Jones was certainly between the devil and the deep blue sea. Right out on the end of the limb, so to speak."

The Air Vice-Marshal blinked just a little at that string of descriptive adjectives, but decided to let them ride without further explanation.

"Yes, Jones was very much in a bit of a spot," he said with a nod. "He had the two halves of paper, but of course he'd had had no time to examine them yet. Fact is, he had no way of knowing whether what he'd heard was true or not. Perhaps those torn halves of paper in his pocket with all the minute writing didn't mean a thing to anybody. In short, it might be best to wad them into a ball and toss them unseen over the side of the police van, and forget the whole thing. Whether they contained things of importance or not would certainly make no difference to the Nazis should those blighters find them on him. The Nazi beggars are thorough, if nothing else. As you say in America, they don't overlook a single bet. They do things automatically, and take care of the questioning part of it later."

"And lots of times they don't even bother with the questioning part!" Dawson spoke up, with a knowing nod. "They may be butchers and murderers, but they aren't anybody's fools."

"Far from it," the Air Vice-Marshal agreed instantly. "So it was very touch and go with Jones. Should he get rid of the stuff and pay attention to saving his own skin? Or should he risk everything until he had a chance to make what he could from the writing on his two torn halves of paper? Well—well, permit me to say that he was a British Intelligence officer, so the decision he made is obvious. He took the chance on keeping the two halves. And for once luck was with him. Unseen by the guard on the van, he managed to wad the two halves of paper—they were very thin sheets—into a ball and hide them in his left armpit under a patch of gummed skin tissue that all agents carry—as you two chaps well know."

The senior officer stopped talking as though waiting for the two air aces to nod. And then he continued on.

"Well, Jones, and those with him, were taken to the town of Opelln inside Germany, and thrown into jail. For thirty hours they had neither food nor water, and four unfortunates died. Or perhaps they were fortunate in being able to die, considering what the others suffered later. Anyway, Jones was unmolested for thirty hours. And you can be sure he made full use of them. He borrowed a pair of thick lens glasses from one of the other prisoners, and using a lens as a magnifying glass, he read what his two halves of paper contained. And I will say right here that it was the most exciting bit of reading that Jones or any other man ever perused. Before his eyes was revealed a good part of what Hitler intended to do. *And*, mind you, exactly what he *has* done since the start of the war! Of course, with only half of it there, Jones was unable to learn definite details. He could only read what he could read, and guess at what the other half contained. But had Jones been able to turn his newly gained knowledge over to us, the—well, I can tell you that the history of this war thus far would have been completely different from what it has been."

"You mean he didn't turn it over to you, sir?" Freddy Farmer blurted out on impulse.

"He didn't have the chance, worse luck!" the other replied, and rubbed one clenched fist into the palm of his other hand. "But he did do the only thing he could do. During those thirty hours he was left unmolested he not only read every one of the unfinished sentences, but he memorized every single word before destroying and disposing of the two torn halves of paper. However, Fate, you might say, was still giving him a black look. At the end of the thirty hours the prisoners were herded into the prison head's office and questioned. Questioned, and knocked about from here to there when they didn't, or couldn't give answers that satisfied their captors. Jones was no better off than any of the others. In fact, it developed that he was worse off. An answer he gave to one question didn't please the Nazi overlord, who lost his temper and struck Jones in the face with his fist. Jones, to save himself from toppling over backwards, flung up both hands, and his right hand unfortunately whacked one of the lesser Nazi officials in the face. And that tore it, of course. Jones wasn't questioned any more. He was promptly jumped on, half beaten to death, and then chained hand and foot, and sent off to a Nazi internment camp."

The senior R.A.F. officer stopped short. His lips stiffened, his two hands bunched into rock hard fists, and there was the bright glint of cold steel in his eyes.

"I need not describe to you the things Jones went through, and suffered, after that!" he finally grated out through clenched teeth. "The so-called routine of a Nazi internment camp is well known all over the world by now. But I come to the end of my part of this story. Six days ago, Agent Jones arrived back in England. He was the mere shadow of the man I sent into Europe over three years ago, but the British spirit, like the American spirit, knows no such thing as defeat. He never gave up. He tried to escape three times, and was caught. He himself says that he'll never know how he managed to go on living from one attempt at escape to the next. But the fourth time he made it. His escape is a hair-raising story in itself, but it's unimportant here, so I won't bother with it. But he did return to England six days ago, and he was able to put down on paper every one of those words he had memorized."

"Stout fellow!" Freddy Farmer cried enthusiastically. "He certainly deserves the Victoria Cross, if ever a chap did. So now all that invaluable information is ours!"

Air Vice-Marshal Leman smiled sadly and shook his head.

"No, Farmer, it isn't," he said slowly. "We only have half of it. And the half we have is practically useless without the other half. Like Jones when he first read it, we can only guess at what the other half reveals. We don't *know*. And guesses in war are quite often as useless as no information at all."

"But, my gosh!" Dawson cried. "You mean, sir, he went through all that for nothing? That he might just as well have tossed the whole thing overboard in the first place?"

"No, not quite, Dawson," the Air Vice-Marshal said. Then, looking over at Colonel Welsh, he added, "I guess you'd better tell the last half of our story, sir."

CHAPTER FOUR
EAST OF DARKNESS

As one man, Dave Dawson and Freddy Farmer swiveled around in their chairs and stared expectantly at the chief of the American Intelligence services. He did not return their look for a moment or two, however. As Air Vice-Marshal Leman had done once or twice, he scowled silently off into space as though thinking up the exact words he wanted to say. Eventually, he seemed to decide on them, and leveled grave eyes at the two youthful airmen.

"Just as Air Vice-Marshal Leman has said," he began slowly, "what little we know of all this Tobolsk business is practically useless without the other half of it. It was the worse kind of luck for Agent Jones not to catch the name of the man he was supposed to contact in Tobolsk. True, Tobolsk is well behind the Nazi lines at the moment. And also, it is quite possible that he may be dead. As a matter of fact, we have every reason to believe that this unnamed man is dead, or at any rate, that he no longer lives in Tobolsk."

"And what do you mean by that, sir?" Dave wanted to know when the other didn't continue at once.

"From certain developments that have recently come to light," the Colonel replied. "From—well, from the American angle of this crazy, mixed up mystery. Contrary to general belief, Yank Intelligence was more than a little active long before the Japs pulled the knife on Pearl Harbor. We knew just as sure as the earth grew little apples that Uncle Sam would be in this war up to his ears before very long. So we did what we could, short of causing the State Department to come down on us with both feet. And—well, to use an expression that groans with age, it certainly is a small world. And there is nothing so baffling, or so helpful, as coincidence. It pops up in the darnedest places, if you get what I mean?"

"I can guess close enough, I think, sir," Dave said with a grin. "Tobolsk again?"

"Take a bow, son," Colonel Welsh grinned back at him. "You just about hit that nail right on the head. Tobolsk again is correct. One of my agents was working with Russian Intelligence until a few days ago. He was actually on the lease-lend end of the business, on the look-out for sabotage along the supply routes leading up through Iraq and Iran from the Red Sea. Well, to get on with the actual story, he was on his way from Baku to Moscow by air when the plane he was in ran smack into a storm, came out of it nobody knew just where, and bumped head on into a flock of German Messerschmitts. And the plane—it was a Russian craft—got shot down. My agent was the only one who came out of the crash alive. He must have been born under a lucky star, because he didn't so much as receive even a goose egg on his head, or a scratch any place.

"The aircraft crashed just before dark, and my agent didn't have the faintest idea where he was, save that he was in the middle of some woods. Anyway, he used his head and put as much distance as he could between himself and the crashed plane. But after a while it got so dark that he couldn't tell but what he might be just going around in circles. At least he realized that he was still in the woods. So he sat down to wait out the night. And lucky for him he did. When daylight came again, he saw to his horror that he was less than a hundred yards from the end of the woods, and an equal distance from a German panzer division obviously camped and resting up from recent action at the front. Naturally, he realized then that he was well behind the Nazi lines. But he still didn't know at what part of the front."

Colonel Welsh paused and smiled grimly.

"There he was smack in the middle of the Germans, and wearing a suit of clothes he had bought in Moscow a month before," he continued presently. "It so happened that he didn't have any money. Nor did he have a gun of any kind. All he had on his person were identification papers that would have slapped him up against a firing squad wall five seconds after the Nazis got their hands on him. So his first job was to destroy all his identification papers. And his second job to make sure the Nazis didn't lay hands on him. Well, we can skip the next few days. He spent all of them, nights included, dodging Nazi patrols, and getting out from under the hand of Death reaching for him. And then came the night of coincidence, we'll call it.

"He was groping his way northward across a field, with the idea of somehow slipping through the Nazi positions to the Russian side, when suddenly the ground seemed just to drop out from underneath him. One instant he was groping his way along, and the next he was out cold as an iced fish. When he opened his eyes again he found himself in the cellar of a bomb and shell blasted farm house. He was stretched out on a smelly mattress, and a couple of thread-bare blankets were over him. He took stock of what was what and realized instantly that he wasn't in Nazi hands. Nazis don't give blankets to prisoners they pick up at night. Anyway, my agent decided to stay right where he was, and wait for whatever was to happen next. And a body full of aches and pains helped him a lot to decide to do just that."

Messerschmitt 109

The Chief of U.S. Intelligence let his words come to a halt, and it was all Dawson and Freddy Farmer could do to refrain from telling him to hurry up and get on with the rest. They held their tongues, however, and waited with pounding hearts and tingling nerves.

"An hour or so later," Colonel Welsh finally continued, "an old man came down into the cellar holding a chipped bowl of some steaming liquid. It proved to be a bitter kind of tree root broth, but just the same it tasted mighty good to my agent. He accepted it, and drank it down without a word. Then he took a good look at this man and saw that he wasn't so old after all. He was no older than my agent, but war had made him look three times his true age. My agent's first questions were concerning what had happened to him, and how he had come to be there. My agent, of course, spoke Russian, but it developed that this man with the root broth spoke English, too. The long and short of it was that in the dark my agent had simply stepped down an uncovered, abandoned well. Why he hadn't broken his neck is something that nobody will ever be able to explain. Anyway, this man, who said he was a Russian, and named Ivan Nikolsk, said that he had found my agent at the bottom of the well. And that he was about to shovel dirt in on top of him, thinking him to be a Nazi, when he saw that my agent's clothes were Russian made. So he hoisted my agent up out of the well and took him down into the cellar. And that was that. Nikolsk simply believed that he was saving the life of a brother Russian. And he'd hide him from the Nazis, who were all about, at least until he'd found out more about the man whom he had pulled from the abandoned well."

The Colonel paused to shrug slightly, and make a little this-probably-sounds-nuts gesture with one hand.

"Well, the two of them started talking back and forth, of course," he resumed his story presently, "and my agent learned a few things about his lifesaver. One, that Nikolsk had been born in Moscow but had lived most of his life in Germany. And two, that Nikolsk had almost lost his life in a railroad train wreck just before the invasion of Poland. And three, that—"

"Good grief!" Freddy Farmer interrupted with a gasp. "The same chap that Agent Jones met!"

"One and the same," Colonel Welsh admitted with a nod. "He told my agent how he had been arrested by the Nazis and thrown into prison, where he almost died as the result of his train wreck injuries. But he survived, somehow. He survived the questioning and beatings he received. And, like Jones, he refused to let a Nazi internment camp finish him off for good. He managed to escape almost three years later and make his way out of Germany, and across German-occupied Poland and German-occupied Russia to the little village of Tobolsk. There he hoped to meet a life-long friend. But he never met him. When Nikolsk finally arrived, his friend, and most of the village's inhabitants, had simply disappeared from the face of the earth. But—"

Colonel Welsh leaned forward slightly and tapped a forefinger on the desk top.

"Ivan Nikolsk had survived things that you could not even put into words, for there are no words in any language to describe them adequately," he said. "But though he came out of it all with his life, he came out of it with only part of his brain. It didn't take my agent long to see that Nikolsk went off the beam completely every now and then. He would be making sense, when suddenly his speech would start rambling all over the place. And even then, almost a year later, he had the certain belief that his friend would return to Tobolsk, and he would be able to see him."

"Did he tell your agent *why* he wanted to see his friend?" Dawson asked eagerly.

"No," Colonel Welsh replied. "That's one of the questions he wouldn't answer, though my agent asked it more than once as he heard more and more of the strange story. It's funny, but though Nikolsk had saved my agent's life, and believed him definitely on Russia's side, he couldn't get it out of his head that my agent might rob him of his great secret. Yes, you're guessing it. Nikolsk's secret knowledge of the Nazi war plan that he had learned while in Germany. Oddly enough, he told my agent every detail of his meeting with Agent Jones. Of how he had torn the secret information in half, given half to Jones, and destroyed the half that he kept. He told my agent all that, but he wouldn't tell him *one word* of what the information was about. And do you know *why*?"

"Didn't trust your agent, obviously," Freddy Farmer spoke up.

"Yes, that's my guess, too," Dawson added.

"No," Colonel Welsh said with a vigorous shake of his head. "True, he didn't tell my agent what his half of the information was because he was afraid of being betrayed. But he wouldn't reveal anything about the other half—*because he had forgotten it!*"

"Forgotten it, for cat's sake!" Dawson exploded. "But—?"

"Just what I am about to explain," Colonel Welsh cut in. "He swore blind that what he knew was of no use at all without the half that he had given to Jones. And to get it all together he had to see either Jones or his friend. He felt that Jones was dead, but—but he still held to the crazy belief that his friend would return to Tobolsk one day, and that together they would place in Joseph Stalin's hands something more valuable than a hundred armored divisions, or a thousand squadrons of aircraft!"

As the echo of the last died away, a tingling silence settled over the room. Dawson had the insane urge to pinch himself hard just to make sure he wasn't sleeping through a very cockeyed dream. He knew, and had seen for himself, many of the upside down things that come out of war. But this dizzy tale was a new high for everything. When he tried to mull it over, and gain some sense from it, it simply made his brain hurt.

"This is certainly something, sir," he mumbled, and gave the Colonel a searching look. "And you are going to say that your agent didn't learn a darn thing, and had to leave it that way? Gosh! I think I would have slung Nikolsk over my shoulder and high-tailed to Moscow as fast as I could, and counted on Joseph Stalin, himself, getting him to talk."

"Don't worry," the Colonel said, with a grim, smile, "my agent thought of that idea, too. But, of course, it was impossible. He even suggested the idea, but Nikolsk would have no part of it. He insisted that what little he might be able to tell Stalin wouldn't help at all. He *Had* to wait for either his friend, or Agent Jones, to turn up. And he was going to park right there in Tobolsk, keeping out of the way of the Nazis, until either of those things happened."

"So I would say," Freddy Farmer spoke up as though talking to himself aloud, "that this friend was the *third* man who possessed part of the original information. Either that, or Nikolsk had sent another copy of all of it to him, in case something should happen to him. And Jones showing up with a torn half would prove to the friend that Nikolsk was finished. And—"

"No doubt the truth of the matter, Farmer," Air Vice-Marshal Leman took up the talking. "This friend was in the know about some of the business, if not all of it, no doubt. But Moscow had received not one single word, which proves what we fear. Namely, that Nikolsk's friend is dead, and will never return to Tobolsk."

Joseph Stalin helped the Soviet Union win World War II, but was responsible for millions of deaths in his country during his rule.

"But there is still Agent Jones!" Dawson cried eagerly.

Colonel Welsh and Air Vice-Marshal Leman exchanged a long look. And it was the R.A.F. Intelligence chief who finally spoke.

"Yes," he said softly. "There is still Agent Jones."

CHAPTER FIVE
DOUBLING FOR DEATH

For a long, long minute Dawson waited for Air Vice-Marshal Leman to continue. But the R.A.F. officer seemed to have said his bit, and that was that. He lapsed into silence and stared fixedly down at his hands folded on the desk. Dave started to put the obvious question, but before his lips could form the words Colonel Welsh broke the silence.

"Yes, there is still Agent Jones," he said. "But it isn't so simple as all that. I mean, it isn't just a question of flying Jones over to Tobolsk and letting him get together with Nikolsk. Ivan Nikolsk has done the disappearing act again. And in addition, we have the very strong hunch that friend Himmler's Gestapo has entered into the picture."

"He's disappeared, sir?" Freddy Farmer choked out. "What blasted rotten luck! But isn't there something that can be done? I mean, have you any idea where Nikolsk might be? And—?"

"One thing at a time, Farmer," Colonel Welsh said with a chuckle, and held up his hand. "Not so fast, son. The thing's a mess right at the moment, but we have hopes."

"Sorry, sir," Farmer said, as the red rushed up his face to the roots of his hair. "But it was a bit of a let-down after getting all warmed up, you know."

"Well, that's the way with war," the American Intelligence chief said with a smile. "But to get on with my story. Just now I jumped ahead. So I'll go back to my agent in Tobolsk. Well, he stayed there in Nikolsk's cellar for four days. By the end of four days he had all his strength back, and falling down the empty well shaft was just an unpleasant memory. During those four days and nights Nikolsk was constantly with him, for the reason that a lot of Germans moved into the village. And from what Nikolsk could see they were there for some mysterious reason. I mean, they didn't camp, and they didn't have much equipment with them. Fact is, they were mostly Gestapo men in uniform.

"So for four days and four nights my agent and Nikolsk hugged that cellar and prayed to their gods that the Germans wouldn't stumble over them. And whenever he had the chance, my agent went to work questioning his new found Russian-friend, but, sorry to say, he didn't even get to first base. The instant those Germans showed up Nikolsk closed up like a clam. Matter of fact, my agent says that he was practically blue with fear most of the time. He seemed to think that the Gestapo boys were after him."

"Were they?" Dawson asked quietly as the other paused.

Colonel Welsh shrugged and dragged down the corners of his mouth.

"Yes and no," he said. "We don't know anything for certain. The next day Nikolsk left the cellar and didn't return. My agent waited a day longer, and then decided that it was time for him to be moving. He had some tattered peasant clothing that Nikolsk had given him, and he slipped out at night and continued his journey northward. In two days he was on the Russian side of the war. And as luck would have it, he bumped into a tank officer he knew. The rest was easy. A plane took my agent to Moscow. And after a day in Moscow he came on down here to London and reported to me. That was last night. When I heard his story I got in touch with the Air Vice-Marshal here. We went into a huddle, and—well, that brings us up to the present moment."

A hundred thousand questions had been leaping around in Dave Dawson's brain. So when the Colonel stopped talking he got the first one out as soon as he could.

"What about your Gestapo hunch, sir?" he asked. "Just how do you mean they've entered the picture? Only because of the Tobolsk business?"

The American Intelligence chief gave an emphatic shake of his head.

"No, not that alone," he said. "My agent stated that he was dead certain that he had been followed in Moscow. And that he is being followed right here in London. True, he's taken all kinds of measures to trip up whoever has been shadowing him. But the lad seems to be very clever. My agent can smell him, you might say. He can even feel eyes watching him. But he hasn't yet been able to get a look at this so-called shadow of his. And you can add to that, sir, eh?"

As Colonel Welsh spoke the last he turned and nodded at Air Vice-Marshal Leman. The R.A.F. officer nodded gravely, and the corners of his mouth tightened slightly.

"Quite!" he grunted, and looked at the two youthful air aces. "The blasted thing is the most incredible mess I've ever bumped up against. Truly fantastic. You'll be sure I've gone balmy when you hear this, but it is the absolute truth. Agent Jones has also been followed ever since he returned! What's more, his flat over on Regent Street has been entered and thoroughly searched at least twice, to his knowledge. And once—though he can't say for sure—a half-hearted attempt to kidnap him was made. At least, he was grabbed during a blackout, and he received a blow on the head that didn't quite stun him. Of course, it might just have been one of those countless blackout accidents. He may have bumped into a couple of skitterish chaps, and they may have got a little bit out of hand.

When the blow didn't stun him, and he wrenched himself free, the two other chaps had disappeared. So there's no way of telling whether it was an accident or the real thing."

"But it must have been an accident!" Dawson spoke up with a frown. "And after what Jones went through, maybe his imagination is playing him tricks. I mean, maybe he just thinks that he's being followed, and thinks that his place was searched. I—"

Dawson cut himself off short, and suddenly felt like kicking himself. A funny look had leaped into Air Vice-Marshal Leman's eyes. And there was also a funny expression on Colonel Welsh's face. Dawson had the instant belief that he had spoken out of turn and put his foot into it.

"You don't agree, sir?" he asked the R.A.F. officer lamely.

The funny light faded from the other's eyes, and he shook his head.

"No, I don't agree, Dawson," he said quietly. "True, I realize that it seems silly to think that the Gestapo got wind of Agent Jones, or Nikolsk, or Colonel Welsh's agent. The whole thing covers a period of about three years, but—well, I have to give credit to Himmler's gang of murderers for one thing, at least. They never forget anything. And they never give up the hunt. How they found out about Ivan Nikolsk, and his connection with Agent Jones, and his connection with the Colonel's agent, are three things we'll probably never learn. But the fact remains that the Gestapo has pulled many things out of thin air in times gone by. It is one of the smoothest working and one of the cleverest organizations in the history of man. So we would be plain blasted fools to brush any thought aside as being impossible of accomplishment. No, far better for us to assume that the Gestapo has wind of what's up, and to make our own plans accordingly."

"Check and double check on that, sir," Dawson said respectfully. "And with your permission, I'd like to withdraw that crazy remark I just made."

"Granted at once, Dawson," the Air Vice-Marshal said with a pleasant smile. "Matter of fact, I really don't blame you for making it. Would have done so myself, if I didn't know all the facts."

A couple of minutes of silence settled over the room, and then it became too much for Freddy Farmer. He inched forward on the edge of his chair, and looked straight at the Air Vice-Marshal.

"Beg pardon, sir," he said, "but may I ask why Dawson and I were ordered to report to you? I mean, is there something we can do to help straighten out the mess? And, if so, I can say for both of us that we're only too eager to try anything."

"Old fire eater Farmer," Dawson said with a chuckle. Then, glancing at the Air Vice-Marshal, he added, "He took the words out of my mouth, sir. I've been wanting to ask that question ever since we came in here."

The Chief of R.A.F. Intelligence didn't reply at once. He looked over at Colonel Welsh, and a special kind of look seemed to pass between them. Then finally, the American officer spoke.

"Yes, we had good reason to send for you two," he said. "And there is a way that you can help—I hope."

"Those last two words don't sound so good, sir," Dawson spoke up with a grin. "You mean, there's nothing definite?"

"No, I don't mean that," the Colonel replied. "I mean—"

The senior officer paused, and scowled heavily as though he were reluctant to let the rest come off his lips.

"No, I don't mean that," he repeated presently. "You two can help us, and more than you realize at the moment. However—well, to give it to you straight, it might turn out to be a dirty trick on both of you. Your war service might suddenly end with a bang, or worse."

Dawson swallowed hard at that remark, but managed to keep a grin on his lips.

"We've flirted with that kind of a situation a couple of times before, sir," he said quietly. "So maybe Lady Luck wouldn't leave us cold all of a sudden."

"Quite!" Freddy Farmer echoed. "At least, it wouldn't be anything new and novel to us, if you know what I mean?"

"I do," Colonel Welsh said with a chuckle. "But it so happens that this would be a new and novel item. That is, unless you've acted as decoys of the real thing in the past?"

"Huh, decoys?" Dawson gulped. "How's that again, sir?"

Colonel Welsh leaned forward and rested his forearms on the end of the desk.

"Obviously," he said, "the thing we want to do, and as soon as we can, is to get Ivan Nikolsk and Agent Jones together. Though Nikolsk has disappeared for the moment, we feel very strongly that he is not very far from Tobolsk. As my agent stated, his one and only aim in life was to meet his friend, or Agent Jones, at Tobolsk. Therefore there is good reason to believe the Gestapo simply scared him into some other place of hiding, and not too far away. So if Agent Jones should go to Tobolsk, the chances are that he would meet up with Ivan Nikolsk sooner or later. My agent and Agent Jones have checked, and the appearance of Nikolsk hasn't changed much. I mean that Agent Jones is certain that he would recognize him at once. And he is also certain that he can fully establish his identity to Nikolsk."

"And our job is to fly Agent Jones to Tobolsk, and land him safely, eh, sir?" Freddy Farmer spoke up excitedly.

"No, definitely not," Colonel Welsh replied evenly. "Your job will be to take the Gestapo boys off the necks of Agent Jones, and get them all wrapped up in the task of chasing you!"

CHAPTER SIX
EAGLES FOR MOSCOW

Had Colonel Welsh calmly pulled out an automatic and fired the whole clip through the ceiling of Room Twelve Hundred, Dave Dawson and Freddy Farmer wouldn't have been half so surprised as they were right at the moment. Like two sitting statues of stone, they froze motionless, and gaped wide-eyed at the Colonel. A billion questions spun around in their brains, but for several seconds neither could have made his lips speak words; not for a million dollars in cold cash.

In time, though, Dawson succeeded in getting his tongue back into working order.

"Sweet tripe!" he exploded. "That is a new one for us! Decoys for the Gestapo rats! Gosh!"

"It doesn't meet with your approval, Dawson?" Air Vice-Marshal Leman put the question with a slight frown.

"Sure, one hundred per cent, sir," Dave came right back at him quickly. "But it was so sudden like—well, it's sort of got me still swinging at thin air. One right on the outside corner that I didn't even see the pitcher let fly."

"Eh, what?" the senior R.A.F. officer grunted with a blank look on his face.

"Another American expression, sir," Colonel Welsh explained immediately. "Dawson means I took the wind out of his sails. Caught him flat-footed off the bag, you might say."

"Oh, yes, quite!" the English officer murmured, but didn't exactly lose his blank look. "Well, I'm glad that you approve, because we are definitely counting on you two for help. If this bit of a mission is completely successful, there's no telling how much it may change the course of the war in our favor, you know."

"If it can be done, we'll both do our best to hold up our end, sir," Freddy Farmer murmured.

"And you can say that again for me," Dawson added his bit. Then, turning to Colonel Welsh, he asked, "What's the plan, sir? Or shouldn't I ask that now?"

"You should, and I'll answer it," the American Intelligence chief replied. "Here is the picture as we've doped it out. You two, whether you admit it or not, are not exactly unknown to the Gestapo. Ten to one the Gestapo knows that you are here in London. In fact, it's almost an even money bet that Gestapo agents in London know that you are here in this office right now."

"Gosh!" Freddy Farmer breathed softly. "That doesn't give a chap a very pleasant feeling. But go on, sir."

"What I'm working up to is this," the Colonel continued. "If the Gestapo has wind of the Tobolsk business, and I'll bet a year's pay that they have, they are going to be just a bit more excited to learn that you two have been brought into the picture. And it is our plan to bring you into the picture right out in broad daylight, so to speak. In other words, the Air Vice-Marshal here, you two, my agent, and Agent Jones and myself are going to have lunch as Simpson's at the Savoy Hotel this noon. Then we are all coming back here for a short while. Tonight you two will travel to Aberdeen in Scotland. There you will board a bomber that will fly you direct to Moscow. When you reach Moscow the Soviet Intelligence will take over. You will disappear from sight, and you will remain out of sight for a bit. Then at the right time you two and a Russian Intelligence officer, who knows every square inch of the Tobolsk area, will take off by plane and head down the front to the village of Urbakh, which is on the Russian side of the front."

The Colonel paused a moment to catch his breath and shift his weight on the chair.

"Meantime," he presently continued, "Agent Jones will also be making a little journey. You see, we hope that you two will be able to draw the Gestapo away from Jones. He will be sneaked out of England by air, and go to Gibraltar, and on to Alexandria, and up through Iraq, and Iran, and up through the Caucasus to the village of Urbakh. There he will meet your party coming down from Moscow, and—well, from that point on, our plan is only general. You, of course, will have to make your own plans from hour to hour, according to how the situation shapes up. The goal, of course, is for all of you to get over into Tobolsk behind the Nazi lines and contact Ivan Nikolsk, and learn what he has to say, in the event you can't get him out of there by air."

"Zowie!" Dawson breathed aloud without thinking. "Just like that, huh? I—Sorry, sir."

Colonel Welsh gave a little wave of his hand to signify that Dawson's comment was taken in the right spirit. In fact, he grinned, and nodded his head vigorously.

"Zowie is right!" he echoed. "I'll admit that the assignment appears so screwy, and dizzy, that a man would be a fool even to give a thought to its turning out even partially successfully. But on the other hand, that's something in our favor in a way. It's such a screwy idea that maybe even the Gestapo wouldn't believe we'd try to pull it off. You see, our hope is that they'll think that you're going to Moscow to turn over valuable information to Soviet Intelligence. In short—well, to be very blunt and brutal, it is our hope that the Gestapo will fall all over themselves trying to *stop you two from reaching Moscow*, and in their efforts will forget all about Agent Jones."

"Well, I wish them luck, I don't think!" Dawson said more cheerfully than he felt. "At any rate, there should be some fun in beating those murdering bums to the punch. Check, Freddy?"

"Quite!" the English-born air ace managed to get out. "I've always wanted to visit Moscow, too."

"Well, our prayers will be that you'll have that opportunity," Colonel Welsh said almost fervently. "If you can shake them off at Moscow, even if they suddenly realize they've been very nicely duped, and guess the real truth, we hope there'll not be enough time for them to do anything about it."

"There's one thing I don't quite catch, sir," Dawson said after a couple of minutes of general silence. "The trip over the Nazi front to Tobolsk. There'll be four of us in the party, and, we sincerely hope, five of us coming out. That's quite a crowd to be charging about behind the German lines, to my way of thinking."

"I agree with you in principle," the American Intelligence chief replied. "But this is one of those occasions where we're banking on the idea of safety in numbers. In the first place, there must be someone along who knows that area like the palm of his hand. That's where the Russian Intelligence officer will come in. He'll know the best place to land, and where to hide the aircraft from prying Nazi eyes. Secondly, there has to be the man to contact Nikolsk. That's Agent Jones, of course. Thirdly, or it should be secondly, Nikolsk will have to be found, and that's where the Russian Intelligence officer will come in handy again. He'll be able to hunt around while the rest of you lie doggo and wait. And lastly, there must be a pilot to fly the plane in, and to fly it out again. That's where you two come in. Double insurance, if you get what I mean?"

"I get it, sir," Dawson said grimly. "You hope that both Freddy and I will fly in, but there *must* be one of us left to fly the ship out, eh?"

"I mean just that," Colonel Welsh said, and there was no smile on his thin face now. "One of you has *got* to come back!"

"And *both* of us will!" Dawson replied instantly.

"Definitely!" Freddy Farmer echoed, and seemed content to let it stay like that.

"Well, that's the picture in more or less detail," Colonel Welsh said with a glance at his watch. "We'll talk over some more of the details again. Right now, though, I guess we've done enough talking. Let's break up this meeting, and think things over. Maybe all of us will have things to add later. That agreeable with you, Air Vice-Marshal?"

"Quite," the senior R.A.F. officer said with a nod. Then, glancing at Dawson and Farmer, "All the luck in the world, you chaps. And I need not tell you how I admire you both, and envy you, too, if you must know the truth. I'd give every one of my stripes of rank to be able to go along with you."

"Thank you, sir," Dawson said for them both. Then, with a point-ed glance at the decoration ribbons under the tunic wings of the Air Vice-Marshal, he added, "And we'd like nothing better than to have you along, sir."

"See here, what about me?" Colonel Welsh snapped with a half grin tugging at the corners of his mouth. "Am I supposed to be an old wom-an, or something?"

"Just Dawson's nasty manners, sir," Freddy Farmer spoke up with a straight face. "He'll never learn. But I can assure you that his words really included you both."

"And how, sir!" Dawson exclaimed hastily. "I figured you'd take that for granted."

"Well, that's a little better!" Colonel Welsh growled in mock annoy-ance. "But you'll never know, Dawson, how close you came to having to pay for that lunch this noon. But of course, I understand, now. So I'll let you off this time, and pay for it myself."

Dawson blew air through his lips, and went through the act of wiping beads of sweat from his brow.

"Boy, did I come close to having to wash a mess of dishes!" he breathed. "Because, if the truth must be known, I've got all of three shillings in my pocket!"

"As though that were unusual!" Freddy Farmer shot at him. "Just name the day when your pay wasn't all spent before you received it."

"Quite!" the Air Vice-Marshal broke into the conversation. "But that's a well known R.A.F. habit, of course. Well, Gentlemen, shall we dis-band, eh, and meet later at Simpson's, what?"

And nobody put forth any objections.

CHAPTER SEVEN
YOU CAN'T SEE DEATH

'**L**ike A black steel snake with a single yellow eye, the "Flying Scotsman" went roaring northward over the steel rails that led to Aberdeen. In their compartment, four cars back from the engine, Dave Dawson and Freddy Farmer tried to lose their thoughts in the newspapers and magazines they had bought before leaving London. But it was just about as easy to do that as it is for a man to shave with an electric razor in a thunder storm.

However, the two air aces stuck grimly to it for well onto two hours, until finally Freddy reached the end of his string. He flung the magazine across the compartment they shared alone, and heaved a long, loud sigh.

"This is without question the balmiest war ever!" he proclaimed with vocal emphasis.

Dawson looked up from his newspaper, nodded, and tossed it to one side.

"At any rate the screwiest one I ever fought in," he said. "So you haven't been reading either, huh?"

"On the contrary, yes," Freddy replied. "But the same blasted paragraph over and over again. I just can't seem to concentrate."

Dave glanced at the thick blinds that covered the windows and smiled faintly.

"I guess nobody could blame you for that, considering," he murmured. "We've been handed some sweet jobs, since we elected to take our own personal swings in this war. And each time has seemed tougher than any of the others. But this—this really is tops for cockeyed assignments. Know something, Freddy?"

"What?"

"We stand *less* chance of pulling this thing off than Mussolini stands of being made King of England," Dave said.

"And don't I know it!" Freddy Farmer groaned. "I swear I don't know who's craziest—Leman and Colonel Welsh for putting the proposition up to us, or us for accepting it. Why, good grief, Dave—"

The English youth seemed unable to continue, so he just left the rest hanging in mid-air, and scowled unseeingly at the single light in the compartment ceiling.

Dave nodded, but didn't speak, because he was thinking the same thoughts as his war pal. And none of them were happy thoughts. True, they would go all out to pull off this miracle that had been dumped in their laps, but he realized in his heart that their chances were thinner

The *Flying Scotsman*

than tissue paper. And every click of the coach wheels on the rail breaks added just another exclamation mark to that thought.

To be truthful with himself, he had actually believed that their chances of success were not much less than fifty-fifty. But that had been during the luncheon at Simpson's. There he had met Agent Jones, and Colonel Welsh's agent, who was introduced by the name of Brown. And something about both men had touched a hidden note within him, and filled him with a savage desire to succeed, and the partial belief that all might come off well, at that. During the luncheon no word, of course, had been spoken of the secret double mission about to be undertaken. But when they had all returned to Air Vice-Marshal Leman's office, they had gone into the whole thing in minute detail. At that time Freddy and he had heard both stories of Tobolsk first hand. And though little was added they had not already heard, hearing the stories from the lips of the men who had gone through it all simply made Dave want more than ever to deliver all the valuable information into the right hands. Maybe it was to help repay Jones and Brown for what they had suffered. Or maybe it was because he believed that success might shorten the war considerably. He couldn't make up his mind which idea appealed to him most. He only knew that, when Freddy and he had finally parted company with the others, he wanted to come through with flying colors this time more than he had ever wanted to in his entire war career.

"Say, Freddy!" Dave suddenly broke the silence. "In case I haven't asked it yet, have you seen any Gestapo lads tagging along after us?"

The English youth shook his head and made a face.

"Not so much as a tiny peep at one," he replied. "And that gets me to thinking. It would be a very bad joke on us if the blighters saw through our little game, and left you and me strictly alone."

"A bad joke, yes," Dawson said with a grin. "But at least we'd be sure to see Moscow. And that was the big attraction in this to you, wasn't it? Or rather, isn't it?"

"Oh, quite!" Freddy snapped at him. "Just to see Moscow. *I'm* really not interested at all in this business about Ivan Nikolsk. But seriously, though, I had a feeling that something might be tried before the train left. But nothing was. Frankly, I'm a little worried."

"Hard-boiled Farmer," Dawson grinned. "Never happy unless he has a fight on his hands. Stop worrying, pal. Something tells me you'll have plenty of chance for action before they ring down the curtain on this job."

"Here's hoping," Farmer mumbled. "But I'm still a little worried. Frankly, I never ask trouble, let alone danger, to come my way. But for once I wish we'd see a bit of it. Such as some beggar coming barging through that compartment door, there, with a gun in his hand."

"What a pretty thought!" Dawson grunted. "Do I get it that you've suddenly got tired of living, pal? Or are you just a little more goofy than usual?"

"Neither!" the other told him shortly. "I simply mean that if something *did* happen to me, I'd feel a little bit better."

"Why, then, just move your jaw this way, my friend," Dave said, and lifted his clenched right fist. "Always glad to oblige an old, old pal."

"The funniest man on earth, for fair!" Farmer snorted. "You'd make millions on the stage—maybe. You nit-wit, don't you get the point?"

"What point, Master Mind?" Dawson shot back at him. "Do you mean that—Oh, oh, I get it. If something happened to us, that would mean that our unseen Gestapo boys were biting at the bait, huh?"

"Splendid!" Freddy Farmer cried in mock joy. "I always knew that that brain of yours would come up with the right answer at least once during your life. Quite! That's exactly what I mean. I wish something would happen that was connected with us. It would certainly make me feel better."

"Well, maybe something will after we get off this train," Dawson said, and stifled a tiny yawn. "Maybe our friends don't like to do things on trains. Maybe ... Hey! We're slowing up for a station stop. Wonder what place it is? Let's have a look. Snap off the light, sweetheart."

Freddy Farmer whipped up his hand, and the compartment was instantly plunged into pitch darkness. Both boys felt their way over to the window and lifted up the blackout blinds. It took a few seconds to accustom their eyes to the even deeper darkness outside. And then they saw that the train was passing the outskirts of a fair sized town, and obviously slowing down for an eventual full stop.

"My guess is that it's Edinburgh," Freddy Farmer said, with his nose pressed against the glass. "We've been on this thing long enough to get there, I fancy."

"There and back, I'd say," Dawson grunted, and squinted his eyes. "There! I just saw a sign, but it could say Broadway and Forty-Second Street, for all I could read. Well, so what, anyway? Let's just say it's Edinburgh, and let it go at that. You can't see the end of your nose in this blackout."

"No, wait!" Freddy Farmer cried out as Dave started to turn away from the window. "It's not Edinburgh. Just some small place. I guess it must be a signal stop. No, it's definitely not Edinburgh yet."

"Okay, that's what I said," Dawson grunted. "Haul down the blinds, and let's put on the light. In this war, I want all the light I can get, when I can get it."

"Half a moment!" Freddy called out, with his nose still jammed against the window glass. "Yes, just as I thought. A signal stop. Two chaps are getting on at the rear. Just saw them now as the train came to a stop. See? And now we're off again!"

All of which seemed to be quite true. The train had stopped for only the fraction of an instant, just long enough to let two passengers swing quickly aboard. And now it was on its way again, and picking up speed fast. After Freddy had hauled the blackout curtains down into place, and snapped on the light again, Dave chuckled and gave a little shake of his head.

"Now what's biting you?" the English-born air ace wanted to know.

"Nothing special," Dawson replied, and stretched out comfortably on the cross-wise seat. "I was just thinking of how a guy does crazy things when there's something on his mind."

"Meaning me, I suppose?" Freddy challenged with a dark scowl.

"Meaning both of us," Dave replied. "Just these last few minutes. The train slowing down, and whether or not it was Edinburgh station. What do we care? We don't. But we act as though the thing were of great importance. See what I mean, pal? When you've got something big on your mind, it's human nature to grab at something small just for a change of scenery, you might say."

"Yes," Freddy Farmer said.

And that was all he said, for at that moment the compartment door was rolled back and the conductor came inside, rolling the door shut behind him.

"Travel vouchers, please, Gentlemen," he said, and held out his hand.

Both Freddy and Dave dived hands into their tunic pockets, and came out with their respective travel voucher slips. They handed them over for inspection, and the conductor stared at them long and hard. Finally he lifted his eyes and looked at them each in turn.

"These aren't in order," he said with a gesture of impatience. "The date stamped on them is too light. I can't read it."

Dawson was tempted to tell him that that was simply his tough luck. But he decided that a train tearing through the blackout was no place for wisecracks. And after all, the conductor was only doing his job.

"They were stamped today, sir," he said instead. "At the Air Ministry. I saw it done myself. So did Captain Farmer. You can take them as being all in order."

That last seemed to be the wrong thing to say. The conductor's eyes flashed and he shot a stern look at Dawson.

"Oh, I can, can I?" he snapped. "Very nice of you to tell me, I'm sure. But I have my orders, and I know what they are. All travel vouchers must be in order for people to travel on *my* train. I'll have to ask you to come along with me and see the Company Inspector, who is in the next to one car back. You can make your explanations to him. And if he says it's all right, then it'll be all right for me."

"And that will be just ducky!" Dawson growled, and got up off the seat. "Okay. If it will take a great load off your mind, my friend, then we'll go back and see the Inspector. But on second thought, let's have the Inspector come see us. What do you say, Freddy, huh?"

"Oh, come off it, Dave!" the English youth growled. "Why make a mountain of it? The chap is just doing his job. So let's go back and straighten it all out with the Inspector. Besides, a bit of a walk wouldn't do either of us any harm."

"For that reason, I agree," Dawson grunted, and stepped through the compartment door that the conductor had rolled open.

Leading the way, he headed for the end of the car, and, unlike in the vast majority of English trains, the end door and passageway that permitted travel from car to car. But just as he was stepping into the next car a figure suddenly appeared out of nowhere directly in front of him, and something blunt and hard was jammed against his chest.

"One sound, and there'll be a dead man under the wheels!" a voice hissed. "Stand right where you are!"

Dave froze stiff, and then was almost knocked off balance as Freddy Farmer came bumping into him from behind. For a split second he half expected to hear the English youth comment volubly on the situation. But he didn't hear a sound. He only felt his pal stiffen, and that was more than enough to tell him that one fake conductor had unquestionably rammed a similar blunt hard object into Freddy's back, and whispered a few words of warning, too.

For a long moment the whole world seemed to stand still for Dave. He knew that he was straining his eyes for a glimpse of the figure blocking his path, but in the bad light he could see nothing but a vague silhouette. Then suddenly he saw the figure's hand reach up and yank hard on the emergency cord. Almost instantly the speed of the train fell off as the engineer up ahead slammed on the brakes. The jolting and jarring lurched Dave forward, but he was prevented from going on his face by the blunt, hard object still digging into his chest.

"I am going to open the side door!" the voice suddenly whispered in his ear. "Get in front of me, and, when I order, jump off the train. But do not try to run away. I will have both eyes on you. And I am a perfect shot, even in the dark. You understand?"

"You've still got the ball, my rat friend!" Dave grated, and took two steps toward the edge of the platform.

The train was almost at a dead stop now, and cool evening air rushed in through the open car door. He stared up at the few stars he could see in the black heavens, and mentally kicked himself hard. Nobody had to send him a telegram to explain what this was all about. He and Freddy had walked right into a perfect trap with their eyes and ears wide open. A neat trick, that conductor stunt. If he ever got out of this he should keep it in mind. A stunt like that might come in handy sometime. In war you never can tell.

But serious as the situation seemed, and unquestionably was, there was still one very satisfying thing about it: an item to which he'd given more than a little thought since Freddy and he had pulled out of the London station. It was the problem of just what they could expect should the unseen Gestapo boys get on their trail. Now he knew. That is, he knew now that it wasn't instant death they could expect. And praise be to the Fates for that small favor. No. Removing Freddy and him from the picture wasn't the goal of those who were after them. It meant that the bait had been perfect. The little play had been acted out to absolute perfection. In short, one Freddy Farmer and one Dave Dawson were wanted *alive*. Yes, very much alive, because it was the information that they were supposed to possess that was wanted most.

And so it wasn't to be murder. It was to be the slightly less important crime of kidnapping. And—

"Jump! And, remember my warning!"

CHAPTER EIGHT
NAZI LIGHTNING

As the night sky suddenly seemed to explode right on top of Dawson's head, and fill his brain with millions of spinning balls of colored light, he had the crazy thought that the order had certainly been a waste of words. And then he went flying out into the darkness. Instinct, and instinct alone, caused him to fling out his hands and bend his knees. For a long moment he seemed to hang motionless in the middle of nothing. And then Mother Earth came up to meet him.

He hit on all fours on the track embankment, and he was too stunned to do anything about it. He could only let his body roll over and over like a barrel rolling downhill, until his progress was stopped short by a heavy clump of thorny bushes. And even then he could still do nothing about it. The balls of colored light were still spinning around inside his head, and to add to it all a couple of hundred heavy caliber guns were sounding off in his brain. Fighting for control of his senses, and gasping for breath, he remained right where he was, too all in and befuddled to care whether school kept or not.

However, he did not remain motionless for very long. Only a moment or two after he had crashed to a full stop up against the thorny bushes, hands of steel came out of nowhere, grabbed hold of him, and yanked him savagely up onto his feet.

"Walk straight ahead, and do not be slow about it!" a voice snarled in his ear. "Cry out, and it will be your last sound in this world! Move along!"

One of the steel fingered hands let go of Dawson, though the other kept a tight grip on the back of his neck. And almost in the same instant he once again felt the familiar pressure of a blunt, hard object jammed into the small of his back. For a split second he hesitated, but only long enough for the sane side of him to point out that any show of resistance at this point would probably be plain suicide. Where Freddy Farmer was, and what had happened to his war pal, he did not know. However, this was not the moment to do anything about it.

And so, choking back the words of blazing anger that rose to his lips, and beating down the mad urge to whirl upon his unknown captor, gun or no gun, he started walking straight ahead through the darkness. In less than a minute his feet told him that he had reached some kind of a country lane. His captor swerved him onto it, and gave him a hard jab with the gun as a signal for greater speed. Dawson obeyed because there wasn't anything else he could do. But most of the spinning balls of colored light had faded from his brain by now, and he was better able to take stock of the situation.

It wasn't a very pleasant picture. In fact, it was most unpleasant, and twice as maddening. Why, not over twenty minutes before Freddy Farmer and he had been tearing along by train toward Aberdeen, *and* complaining of the fact that things were going along too smoothly. Well, Freddy had surely got his wish. Things had happened, and happened with a bang. There was no doubt, now, that Gestapo agents in London had grabbed at the bait thrown out by Colonel Welsh, and taken it hook, line, and sinker. So what?

So a well planned stunt had back-fired almost before it had been put into execution. And it had been done so easily and so simply, too. That was what made Dawson see red as the steel fingers and the business end of a gun prodded him along a night-shrouded country lane. Nobody had to explain to him that the two Gestapo agents had boarded the train at that whistle stop. And nobody had to explain to him, either, that they had timed every move to perfection. The emergency cord had been yanked at the right moment so that the train would come to a stop at the right place. The way in which "Steel Fingers" shoved him forward was proof in itself that this country lane was well known to him, and a definite part of this kidnapping escapade. Yes, it had been simple, and a cinch. Like rolling off a log. Or better, rolling off a railroad track embankment.

At that moment the shrill sound of a locomotive whistle came to Dave's ears. And almost immediately he heard the distant snorting and puffing of the Flying Scotsman getting under way again. Those sounds chilled his heart just a little bit more, and fanned into flame the smouldering anger in his breast. He could feel his face grow hot with the shame of having walked into this little trap so doggone blindly. He wondered how Freddy was taking it, if his pal was pleased that his wish for action had been granted. But more than that, he wondered how Freddy was, and *where* he was.

As though the gods of war had simply been waiting for him to start wondering in earnest about Freddy Farmer, the steel fingers gripping him by the back of the neck suddenly tightened and jerked him to a halt. He was spun around to face the shadowy figure of his captor, but the barrel of the gun was quickly moved from the small of his back to a point on his chest directly over his heart. And the harsh voice spoke again—almost invitingly, it seemed to him.

"Don't move a muscle! Not a muscle!"

Dawson remained motionless as ordered, but he strained his eyes in the darkness for a glimpse of his captor's face. He might just as well have tried to study a sheet of black paper at the bottom of a coal mine at midnight. He could only see that his captor wore a snapped down brim hat pulled low over his eyes. The face could be that of a Jap, for all he could tell.

However, he knew that the man was not a Jap. The voice had disproved that. Yet, at the same time, the sound of that harsh voice had built up the fires of rage in Dave, for the simple reason that he felt sure that his captor was *not* a German. At least he felt pretty sure. He had the strong belief that his captor was English. The harsh voice had the Midlands twang, that is so much like the New England twang. Of course, he might be dead wrong, but—

The rest of his rambling thought flew off into oblivion as two shadows suddenly emerged out of the gloom, and he saw that one of them was Freddy Farmer, and, right behind his pal, the man in a train conductor's uniform.

"You okay, Freddy?" he asked quickly.

For an answer to his question the gun was practically shoved through his ribs, and a hand smacked him across the face.

"Silence!" Harsh Voice rasped at him "One more sound *will* be your last!"

"I'm all right, Dave," Freddy Farmer said, almost as an echo to the threat of violence. "I saw H-Sixty-Four drop off the train, so these blighters won't last very long."

The last caused Dave to blink hard in the darkness. For three or four seconds he wondered what in the world Freddy meant, and if his pal had received too hard a crack on the head. Then in a flash the truth came to him. And almost in the same instant it was confirmed by the one with the harsh voice.

"What's that?" the blurred figure demanded. "Who is this H-Sixty-Four?"

Dawson leaped at the opening and chuckled softly in spite of the risk.

"You'll find out, and fast, tramp!" he snapped. "Think we would have fallen for that conductor gag if we hadn't been expecting it, or something like it?"

"Quite!" Freddy Farmer quickly took up the play. "And the laugh is really on you chaps. *It's* on its way to Aberdeen now. If you don't believe me, then search us. And—Did you hear that, Dave?"

Dawson started to open his mouth, but a hard hand was clamped over it, and the gun barrel felt like a knife in his chest. A voice whispered softly, but it didn't come from the owner of the hand clamped tightly over his mouth. It came from Freddy Farmer's captor.

"Get along with them to the place! Stohl will get the truth out of them. If your swine makes a sound, give him one and carry him on your shoulder. We've got to get away from here, whether they're lying or not. I don't like it!"

"Yes, this is Stohl's business," the one with the harsh voice hissed back. "Our job is only to deliver these two. Come on!"

And then began another walk up the night-shrouded lane, although it could hardly be called a *walk*. Steel Fingers forced Dave along at a rapid rate, and the gun that had returned to the small of his back was sufficient urging to make him hold the fast pace. However, there was just a little more joy in his heart now. Just a little, to be sure. Freddy and he were still helpless prisoners, but Freddy's fast thinking had at least changed the picture a little. It had put a little fear in the minds of their captors. Or at any rate, it had caused them to believe that their plan had not turned out exactly the way they had expected. Obviously, their job had been to nail Freddy and himself. A third person hadn't been counted on. And Freddy Farmer's lie had touched off the jitters a little bit, anyway. And when your enemy starts getting the jitters, there's no telling what can happen.

Maybe yes, maybe no! But Dawson clung hard to that tiny thread of hope as he was shoved and prodded forward along the night-shrouded road. Several times he was tempted to trip himself up purposely, and take his chances of his captor tumbling down on top of him. But the thought of Freddy Farmer and the conductor right behind curbed the crazy urge. If just Harsh Voice and he were alone—But, of course, the conductor had a gun, too. And besides, there was no way of letting Freddy know that it had been no accident.

"Save it!" he told himself grimly. "Play it out the way it's going. One thing is certain. These tramps don't *want* to kill us. Which, of course, means that they've received orders *not* to. So just bide your time—and maybe it'll come along!"

And so, with the decision fixed firmly in his mind, he let himself be led through the night for another good ten minutes. At the end of that time he was suddenly guided off the country lane to the right, and into some woods. But once again it became instantly evident how thoroughly this kidnapping had been planned. He didn't go bumping into any trees or bushes. On the contrary, there was a winding path under his feet, and he was guided forward at practically the same speed, as though his captor had the eyes of a cat.

And then without warning the woods stopped and opened up into a clearing. In the center of the clearing was a small house. Rather, it appeared to be little more than a shack. Not so much as a pin point of light showed anywhere, but of course that didn't mean a thing. In the British Isles they *observe* the blackout, and constantly.

Dawson was led right up to the front door of the shack, and then yanked to an abrupt halt. Almost before he could realize what was taking place, his captor whipped out with his gun and rapped sharply three times on the door. Then the gun came right back to the small of Dawson's back. Standing perfectly still with his gaze fixed on the night-shrouded door, Dawson heard Freddy Farmer and his captor come panting up to a halt. And then there was the sound of the door opening, although no light cut through into the darkness. The door simply swung all the way back, and an instant later the black oblong where the door had been spoke words.

"Come in, at once! Don't just stand there, fools!"

The sound of that voice in the darkness sent a little cold shiver rippling through Dawson. It was gone in an instant, but not before he was dead sure that the words had come from a Nazi throat. He had had the feeling all along that his captor and Freddy's conductor were English. Yes, English-born rats who would sell out their country for gold. History has proved time and time again that there are rats like that in every nation on the face of the earth. But the man who had spoken from the darkness was one hundred percent Nazi breed. The tone of his voice indicated as much, and Dave was sure that one look at his face, the set of his eyes, the slope of his forehead, and the width of his jaws would be the final proof.

And that final proof was revealed no more than twenty seconds later. Just time enough for Freddy and himself to be herded in through the doorway, for the door to be slammed shut, and a match touched to the wick of an oil lamp on a table in the middle of the room. For a moment the sudden change from pitch darkness to light threw Dawson's eyes all out of focus. Presently, though, he was able to adjust his vision, and get his first look at his captors.

His hunch was correct. The faces of the pair that had boarded the Flying Scotsman at that signal stop were typically beefy British red; the faces of men who spent most of their lives outdoors in a climate that could be damp and clammy one day, and windy and icy the next. And the third man, the one who had spoken from within the night-shrouded doorway, was thoroughly German. His face had that moon-shaped, brutish look, his eyes the look of something vile and treacherous. And the very air about him smelled of things foul and evil.

"Good!" the man suddenly broke the silence, and smirked with pleasure. "Those are the two. For once you did not bungle my orders. I am delighted. Put them in those chairs, and keep your eyes on them. You had no trouble, no?"

The two kidnappers hesitated, and glanced at each other. Then quick as a flash Dawson laughed aloud.

"Nope!" he said. "No trouble at all—*yet!*"

The one who had been referred to as Stohl half whirled and fixed blazing gimlet eyes on Dawson.

"Hold your tongue, swine!" he snarled. "You will speak when I order you to. Now, you, answer my question!"

A tiny note of worry was mixed up in the snarl directed at the two kidnappers, and hope began to surge up in Dawson. He and Freddy had been shoved down into a couple of chairs, and they had a good look at the beefy-faced pair. At that moment the one in conductor's uniform spoke. He seemed to have to force the words off his lips one at a time.

"No trouble, *Herr* Stohl," he said. Then, stabbing his eyes at Freddy, he continued, "But that one there spoke of an H-Sixty-Four dropping off the train. And he said, also, that something was on its way to Aberdeen now. They dared us to search them, but we did not wish to waste time. I—perhaps there is some place you wish me to go now, *Herr* Stohl? I mean—"

"I know what you mean, you swine, you sniveling dog!" the Nazi exclaimed. "I knew you had not the courage of a snail. So you wish to run away now, eh? You are afraid of your own shadow, is it not so? Bah! I have no use for jellyfish like you. So *go!*"

As the last word left his lips the Nazi's hand streaked into his jacket pocket and out with the speed of lightning. Dawson's eyes saw the revolver with the silencer fitted to the barrel. And his ears heard the faint *pop* that it made. But not until the man in conductor's uniform turned slowly around and then crumpled to the floor in a motionless heap did his brain actually grasp what had happened.

"And *that* for a swine dog with water for blood!" Stohl rasped, and swung his gun to point straight at the other kidnapper's chest. "Well, Bixby? You would like to join the swine, eh?"

CHAPTER NINE
TNT TWINS

For five long seconds the whole world seemed to cease revolving, as the man addressed as Bixby went white as a sheet and struggled frantically for the use of his tongue. His eyes went mad with fear, and sweat poured down his face. He had his own gun in his hand; but he seemed not to realize that fact. His fear-streaked, glassy eyes were fixed upon Stohl as though the Nazi were some kind of a powerful magnet that he could not resist.

And then without warning the half screamed words came out with all the turbulent fury of flood waters rushing through a broken dam.

"No, no! Please don't shoot me! Don't shoot me, *Herr* Stohl! I am not like him. I want to stay. I want to help. I swear it to you. Do not shoot me, for Heaven's sake!"

The Nazi gave him a long, hard stare, and then smirked broadly.

"Good, then!" he rasped. "But see that your tongue does not make the same mistake as did that dead fool's. Now, what about this H-Sixty-Four? And what about something on its way to Aberdeen?"

Fear still had the man named Bixby by the throat, and the words he spoke sounded like small stones sliding down a tin roof.

"I know nothing about it but what he said," he finally choked out, with a gesture toward the dead man. "I don't know what it all means. Those two, there, can perhaps tell you. I do not know."

The Nazi scowled for a moment, as though he were debating whether to believe Bixby or not. Then he muttered something under his breath, and half swung around to Dawson and Freddy Farmer.

"Very well, then!" he rasped out. "You will tell me what it was all about, eh?"

Dave hesitated a moment to give Freddy Farmer a chance to say what he might have to say. But the English youth remained silent. Dave glanced at him out of the corner of his eye, and saw that Freddy seemed not to have heard the question. The English-born air ace sat half slumped in the chair, with his eyes fixed on the oil lamp of the table, and a completely uninterested and almost vacant look on his sun and wind-bronzed face.

"Can't you guess?" Dave snapped, switching his gaze to the Nazi's face. "Do you think United Nations Intelligence is as dumb as your Gestapo? Figure it out for yourself. It's simple!"

The Nazi didn't like that, and the savage, animal look that leaped into his eyes made Dave just a little bit sorry that he had been so flip with his reply. This Nazi was obviously the kind of snake who could take so much, and then would go off the deep end, regardless of the consequences of his hair trigger temper. However, the German held his boiling rage under control, and did no more than take a bead with his silencer fitted revolver on a point squarely between Dawson's eyes.

"Your tongue is begging for your death!" he said in a voice trembling with suppressed rage. "Speak again that way, and it will be granted! Now, take your choice!"

Dave Dawson looked straight into the muzzle of certain death, and at the same time forced a grin to his lips.

"Maybe it's *you* who has the choice, *Herr* Stohl," he said slowly and deliberately. "Your agents have letters and numbers to identify them, don't they? Well, so do our agents. And if that doesn't mean anything to you, here's the tip-off. What you want, my pal and I *were not carrying on us.* H-Sixty-Four had it, see, Stohl? *But* if anything happened to us, H-Sixty-Four was to pass it on to a *fourth* person on that train, and come to our rescue. That's right! I said *rescue!* In case you don't know, British Intelligence thinks there are too many of your kind on this island. They are doing something about it. And so—"

Dawson didn't finish the rest. He had the sudden fear that he had spoken too much nonsense already. So he left the rest hanging in thin air. The Nazi bored him with his eyes, and in those eyes Dawson saw clearly the shadows of worry, doubt, and frank disbelief. And as frank disbelief gradually blotted out the other two Dawson realized that death was coming closer and closer. This Stohl was no fool. What Dawson had said had worried him at first, but now he was beginning to see through it and recognize it as just so many useless words. Which it was.

"A very good try, *Herr* Captain Dawson!" the German suddenly barked. "Yes, of course I know you, and your swine comrade, too. In fact, *I* know everything. You fools—to think you can keep secrets from the Gestapo! I know that you were on your way to Aberdeen. I know that at Aberdeen a British bomber is awaiting you. And I also know that the bomber is waiting there to fly you to Moscow. But neither you nor your swine comrade will ever reach Moscow!"

Dawson's heart was a solid lump of ice in his chest. He wanted to believe that he hadn't heard a single word spoken. He wanted to believe that it would have been absolutely impossible for Gestapo agents in London to learn even that much of Freddy's and his mission. He wanted to believe that he was simply thinking of those things in his mind, and so shouldn't take the words as having come from the lips of the Nazi, Stohl.

Sure! He *wanted* to believe all that. But he couldn't! More than once in the past had he been in situations where the Nazi Gestapo had learned things that were believed to be cast iron secrets. More than once had a supposedly loyal Englishman, or American, in an important post, turned out to be nothing but a black-hearted Nazi. And so to hear those words from Stohl's lips did not shock him so much as sicken him and stir up the bitterness of war within him. What pair of ears in Air Ministry had heard of this part of the plan, he would probably never know. But that made little difference now. That is, save for one terrible possibility. That a Nazi pair of ears had heard *all* of the plan. That even now Jones was a prisoner, and—

"But no, you dope!" his brain screamed at him. "Catch hold of something, and stop going haywire. If the Nazis knew *all*, why should they bother about Farmer and you? They wouldn't! Agent Jones would be their man, because Agent Jones is the one key to the success of this whole thing. He alone is the one to contact Ivan Nikolsk. So snap out of it, and just let this Nazi go on fishing!"

His thoughts boosted his spirits, and gave him some encouragement and hope—but not a terrible lot. The fear still lingered that the Nazis *did* know all about the Tobolsk business. Yes, the fear that possibly the Nazi plan was to put Freddy and him out of the picture, just in case. Right! Just to make *sure!*

Brushing the taunting thoughts from his mind, Dawson eyed the Nazi coolly.

"All right, have it your way," he said evenly. "So we don't see Moscow. But *that* doesn't matter, *now*. Like you, *Herr* Stohl, we play the part assigned to us, and let *others* do the rest. I'm not denying a thing. You win this round. My pal and I seem to have been put out of the picture. Okay. In war a man has to take his chances—and trust to luck."

As Dawson finished speaking he half shrugged and made a faint gesture with one of his hands. But inwardly he was praying hard, and as he studied the Nazi's face he had the feeling that his prayers were being answered a little. His complete about-face wasn't setting so well with *Herr* Stohl. The German obviously hadn't expected so sudden an admission of defeat, and it puzzled him not a little. He searched Dawson's face for some hidden answer, and unconsciously let his gun sag until it was pointed toward the floor.

That was the moment for which Dave was waiting, to stake all on one swift lightning-like bit of action. However, the Yank-born air ace, in his own eagerness to befuddle Stohl slightly and get him off guard for the moment, had forgotten one very important item. And that item happened to be Freddy Farmer, in the flesh. Freddy was playing his own kind of game, too. And even as Dave coiled his muscles for a diving leap at *Herr* Stohl's legs, Freddy Farmer was way out ahead of him.

From a man half slouched, down in a chair, the English youth became a roaring tornado of savage action in nothing flat. Dave had just a split second in which to see Freddy's arm move like a striking cobra; to see something sail out of his hand. And then the oil lamp on the table went crashing off and down onto the floor. Just what else Freddy Farmer did, Dawson didn't have time to see. He didn't, for the simple reason that putting his own Commando training and actual experience to good use required all of his attention.

Like a shot from the mouth of a gun, he hurled himself up onto his feet, and off the floor, to sail straight forward and low down. He heard Stohl cry out in alarm and rage. Then Dave's shoulder crashed into his knees, and the German went over backward and down like a felled ox. But even as Dave crashed into the Nazi, he kicked outward with his left foot. It was a case of nailing two birds with one stone, so to speak. And he succeeded. His booted left foot caught the half stunned Bixby in the stomach, and doubled him over with pain split seconds before he could snap out of his trance and make use of the gun he held in his hand.

Then down on top of *Herr* Stohl crashed Dawson. He tried to protect himself as much as possible, but his momentum was terrific, and new and brighter stars began to whirl about as his forehead slammed down on the boards. Every nerve and muscle in him went limp and jelly-like. He was sure he heard the faint *pop* of the Nazi's revolver, and thought he felt a white hot spear of flame cut across the top of his shoulder. But he was too stunned to be sure of anything, save the fact that the whole wide world was now a glowing red, and that acrid smoke was driving every ounce of air out of his lungs, and burning their walls to a crisp.

In a vague, abstract sort of way he realized that the oil lamp crashing down onto the floor had sprayed burning oil in all directions, and that the floor was fast becoming a seething sea of fire. He realized all that, and even saw it with his own dazed eyes, but his whole body seemed to be clamped fast in a gigantic vise, so that he couldn't move an inch.

Then suddenly some great weight crashed down on top of him. In the same instant a gun roared out sound. The weight dropped down on his back, went limp, and rolled off him onto the floor. The sudden bit of mysterious action seemed to release a hidden spring within him. Strength rushed back into his body, and his muscles ceased to be limp any more. Hardly realizing that he had done so, he scrambled up onto his feet, and leaped back from a tongue of flame. He crashed into Freddy Farmer, but the English youth grabbed hold of him and checked him from tumbling down onto the floor again.

"This way, Dave!" he heard Freddy shout. "Nice work, old chap. I'm sure he was dead before he even fired his gun. Broken neck, you know. And good riddance. Come along, pal!"

The words made little sense to Dave, but his aching lungs were too empty of air to make questions possible. Besides, Freddy Farmer had him by the arm and was dragging him over to the door of the shack. He had just time enough to glance back and see the still form of Bixby, with a bullet hole square in the middle of his forehead, the still, motionless figure of Stohl with his head twisted around in a horrible position, and the seething, hissing pool of burning oil that was lapping its way across the floor boards. Then Freddy Farmer yanked open the shack door, and they both leaped through and out into the dark night.

"Keep going!" the English youth barked sharply as Dave started to pull up to a halt. "That whole blasted thing is going to be a torch of flame in no time at all. And we haven't time to answer questions for a lot of Air Raid Wardens and Auxiliary Police chaps. We want to get away from here fast!"

Dave didn't bother to question that because it had all made good sense on his spinning brain. So he simply gulped night air into his aching lungs and raced along through the night at Freddy's side. No less than a thousand times, it seemed, they tripped over tree roots, rocks, and shrubs, and almost went flat. But somehow they both managed to keep their feet, and presently they broke through some shrubbery and out onto the smoothness of a well paved road. There they pulled up to a halt by silent mutual agreement. And by the same kind of agreement they slumped down by the side of the road and fought to regain their breath.

Finally Freddy Farmer was able to talk without wheezing out the words.

"Well, that's a score for our team, what?" he said. "A bit risky while it lasted, though. Anyway, those three dirty blighters will have no more to do with this war, thank heaven!"

"Me, I say, thank *you*!" Dave corrected. "Sweet tripe! You sure are learning fast, pal. You were way ahead of me that time. Fact is, I'm still not sure just what did happen. What about what broken neck? And who shot that Bixby?"

"Guilty," Freddy Farmer said grimly. "He was just about to have a go at you when I put an end to his dirty work. I guess you must have stunned yourself going down on that Stohl. But what a beautiful tackle, Dave! Don't ever try it on me, even in fun. I wouldn't want my neck broken the way his was. Just as I got hold of the gun, and was turning around, I saw him fire. But I'll swear he was stone dead at the time. Well, it looks like we both had the same thought at the same time, eh? I'd been playing doggo for what seemed like hours, waiting to have a go at that oil lamp."

"With what, I want to know?" Dave asked. "I thought I saw something fly out of your hand. What was it?"

"A rung of the chair they'd pushed me into," Freddy said quietly. "Rickety old thing, it was. Blessed wonder it held me up. The two of them were so interested in you, old chap, they didn't even see me work it loose. Well, they're done with, and we've got to be getting along. When the Flying Scotsman arrives at Aberdeen without us—"

"It will, anyway," Dave said, and grabbed hold of Farmer's arm, "so one more question won't change anything. About the gun you said you got hold of—what one?"

"This one," the English youth, replied and held out a small bore automatic. "It's that conductor beggar's, of course. When he fell to the floor this slid out of his hand. Nobody paid any attention to it. But I did. Oh, quite! That's what I had my eye on all the time. It, and that oil lamp on the table. And thanks to your bit with *Herr* Stohl, I had the chance to dive for it and get it in time. Good gosh! Did you think I simply planned to fight my way out of that mess with my bare hands?"

Dave Dawson chuckled, gave him a friendly slap on the back, and got up onto his feet.

"Darned if you couldn't have done that, too, pal," he said. "Like I always say, just the guy to have along when you get into a jam. And, Freddy, that *was* a jam! A tough one. Remind me next time, same which I hope there won't ever be. Because next time it'll be my turn to be the fair-haired hero. Yes sir, Freddy! You're something. And I don't mean maybe!"

"Rot!" the English youth snorted, but his face beamed with pleasure. "After all, it took the two of us to get the two of us out of it. And, frankly, I didn't think much of our chances for a while. That—that double talk of ours didn't make any impression on that Stohl. He's no fool."

"Was no fool," Dave corrected, and drank in the night air. Then, half turning, "Boy! See the reflection of those flames. Ugh! A horrible end for rats, even if they were rats. Let's get going. But heck! Which way? I haven't the faintest idea where we are."

"I think I know," Freddy Farmer spoke up, and pointed along the road to his left. "Ahead, there, is a town called Leadburn, unless I'm completely mistaken. This is the Old North Road, anyway. I'm positive of that. But let's go off here to the left. It's toward the north, anyway. We'll hunt up the Military Commandant of the first town we come to, and get him to loan us a car."

"What a sweet hope!" Dave grunted. "We just ask him and he agrees to ..."

"Of course not, stupid!" Freddy Farmer snapped. "I say, you *must* have got quite a blow on your head, to think I'd try anything that silly."

"Okay," Dave sighed as he dropped into step. "Just what kind of magic do you intend pulling to get a Military Commandant to loan a car to a couple of strangers with dirty uniforms, and dirtier faces, too? And in war time?"

"You just don't know me, that's all," Freddy commented with a chuckle.

"Know you?" Dave snorted. "If *I* don't, then *who* does?"

"You!" the English youth shot right back at him. "But don't throw that brain of yours out of gear wondering, my good fellow. I'll explain. It will be all very simple. The telephone, see? A telephone call to the Air Ministry. And if the Air Ministry doesn't clear the fog of doubt and suspicion over us—why then—"

"Why then we walk to Aberdeen," Dawson interrupted. "But take a bow, son. You've really got something there, at that. My error."

"Granted," Freddy Farmer said sweetly. Then with profound relief echoing in every word, he said, "Well, anyway, they took good hold of the bait. And what's more, we landed them right into the boat. Now we shouldn't bump into any more trouble until we leave Moscow for Urbakh, and Tobolsk. If even then."

"Yeah, sure," Dawson said absently. "But me, I've learned never to count on even a sure bet in this crazy war. Three Gestapo rats are dead and gone out of the picture for us. But there are lots and lots of other Gestapo rats still alive and kicking. And between you, me, and this town I hope we reach darn soon, I've a hunch that we've only seen a little of the *beginning* of trouble on this cockeyed mission."

And as the echo of Dawson's comment died away, the gods of war in their high places of hiding nudged each other, grinned wickedly, and nodded their heads in complete and absolute agreement with all that had come off Dave Dawson's lips!

CHAPTER TEN
EASTWARD TO WAR

A cold, dirty grey fog hung over the Royal Air Force Depot, at Aberdeen, Scotland, like a soggy blanket just about ready to drop. Ceiling was about eight hundred feet, and visibility was about a third of a mile, if you had good eyes. Far to the east the sun of a new day was dawning. But you would never have been able to tell by looking in that direction. There was nothing but dirty grey fog stretching out to the four horizons. Only there weren't even any horizons. There was just fog, and more fog.

The state of the weather, however, had not put any damper on plans for R.A.F. activity. At every dispersal point about the Depot field were aircraft of all types being made ready for the day's aerial smash against the Axis forces on the Continent. Planes of every description, ranging from sleek, powerful Supermarine Rolls Royce "Merlin" powered Spitfire Mark V's to the gigantic death dealing Lancaster bombers. And swarming all over them, like so many industrious ants, were the R.A.F. mechanics. The riggers, the fitters, the armorers, and the countless other members of the ground crews that keep the planes in the air.

Over in one corner of the field, though, was a lone Vickers "Wellington" bomber. And grouped under one of its huge wings were five airmen dressed for the skies. Three of them wore R.A.F. uniforms, but Dave Dawson and Freddy Farmer still wore their U.S. Army Force uniforms, though they were not in the best of condition as a result of the boys' recent experience with three worshipers of Hitler, who wouldn't be around any more.

As a matter of fact, it had been their torn and mud-smeared uniforms that had come close to delaying their arrival at the Aberdeen R.A.F, Depot indefinitely. Following Freddy Farmer's plan of action, they had walked three miles along the Old North Road to a town which did turn out to be Leadburn, just as the English-born air ace had guessed. Patroling Home Guards stopped them, and after considerable argument they were taken to the quarters of the town's Military Commandant. That gentleman was awakened from a deep sleep, and he didn't like it at all. He didn't even like it a little bit. And being that kind of an officer, he felt that the two youths should be tossed into the local clink for the rest of the night, and their case looked at in the broad light of day.

But at that point both Dave and Freddy went to work on him, so to speak, much to the silent amusement of the Home Guards. At any rate, they convinced the Commandant that he should phone the Air Ministry. He did, and that changed everything, instantly. The boys couldn't hear what was said at the other end of the wire, but they didn't have to. The sullen annoyance in the Commandant's face changed at once. His eyes widened to saucer size, and his face turned a deep brick red color that went right up into his hair. He almost got his tongue tangled up in his teeth telling the person at the other end of the wire that he would "do that at once." And when he finally hung up, his forehead was dotted with beads of nervous sweat.

And so the boys got action, plus! In less time than it takes to tell about it the Commandant's own car was turned over for their use. And they were given a Corporal, who knew the roads well, to handle the wheel. And that was exactly what the Corporal did, and then some. He was ordered to make the run north to Aberdeen Depot as fast as he could, and hardly had he shifted gears before both boys realized the man planned to do even better than that. He was indeed an expert driver, but even experts break their necks sometimes. And what worried Dave and Freddy as they shot northward through the night was that the driver would not only break his own neck, but theirs as well!

Lady Luck rode with them, however. And in due time they passed through the Aberdeen Depot gates, and were conducted over to the Depot Commandant's office. He had been waiting for them, and getting new grey hairs with every passing minute. Of course the Flying Scotsman had long since arrived at the station, and when they were not found aboard, the Commandant had more or less taken it as his personal responsibility. And so his joy was great and his relief unbounded when finally the two youths did show up. He took them under his wing at once, and got them a good meal and something hot to drink. Then he chatted with them for a bit, and it was all the two youths could do to stop from grinning in his face. Naturally, the Commandant knew nothing, save the fact that they were to be flown to Moscow, and so naturally he dropped a casual question here and there in an effort to add to his knowledge.

But neither Dave nor Freddy were having any of that. As a matter of fact, if either of them was tempted to give their host a tip as to the nature of their mission, they had only to think of that little business aboard the Flying Scotsman to be easily able to kill such an intention right then and there. If German agents had big ears in London, they would certainly have big ears in Aberdeen. And the conviction that of course there weren't any Nazi agents way up there in Aberdeen was just about the stupidest idea one could have. Nazi agents are like cockroaches. You'll find them around, no matter how many you kill, until you've found the nest and burned it out. And the Gestapo nest was in Berlin.

However, the hour or two with the Depot Commandant passed pleasantly enough. And then the pilot, navigator, and radioman of the Moscow-bound bomber reported at the Commandant's office. The pilot was a Squadron Leader named Freehill, and the ribbons under his wings proved that he had won his rank the hard way. The navigator was a Flight Lieutenant named Parsons, and he had a ready smile and a hearty handshake that made both Dave and Freddy feel glad that he was going to be along on the flight to Moscow. The radioman was a cheery-faced sergeant named Dilling, who looked as if he should be on the vaudeville stage rather than inside a Wellington bomber. All three of them seemed rather mysteriously tickled about this coming flight to Moscow, but it was not until later, when they were all taking it easy under the Wellington's wing, while the twin Bristols were warming up, that Squadron Leader Freehill explained the reason for their secret joy.

"This aerial taxi business has almost got us down," he said out of a clear blue sky. "But not this trip we're to make with you chaps. You're a blessing, if there ever was one, or two, rather. It should be a bit of all right this time, I'm sure."

"Here's hoping, anyway," Dave said with a grin. "But I don't know what you're talking about. What do you mean, this trip is to be different?"

"A difference of about two thousand miles, for one thing," the other replied with a chuckle. "And a good chance to see a Jerry or two, for another. Or at any rate, so I hope. You see, most times we're blasted chauffeurs for some war correspondents, or some brass hats, or political big wigs, headed for Moscow to chat with Stalin and all the lads. Very valuable cargo, you know. And we must get them there without grey hairs, or them getting their feet wet. So we have to fly a course north to within six hundred miles of the Pole, and then around the tip of Norway and down into Russia through Murmansk and Leningrad. Like flying through an ice box. Terribly cold. And no end boring, too. Except for Parsons, here. He's kept pretty busy making sure we don't end up in Greenland or some such other place."

"Quite!" the navigator echoed with a faint chuckle. "Takes me a week to rest my poor brain after one of those thirty-two hundred mile hops. No fun at all, really. You two chaps we are taking across as the crow flies. Wouldn't be at all surprised if a Jerry or two came up for a look at us. They're frightfully worried about R.A.F. planes over their heads these days, you know."

"Don't I hope a few do come up, though!" Sergeant Dilling spoke up with a broad grin. "It's so long since I had a Jerry in my sights I'm worried for fear I won't be able to recognize one of the beggars. It will be wonderful, no end, to spill one of the blighters down in a mess of flames. At least it will give me the feeling that at last I'm doing something to earn my pay."

"Well, we want to get to Moscow all in one piece," Dave said with a little laugh, "but I can't say that I'd be too mad if a couple of Messerschmitts did put in an appearance. How about the weather, Squadron Leader? Does this stuff go very far out?"

The Wellington's pilot grinned, and winked one eye.

"Far enough out," he replied. "According to the latest reports we'll have it all the way to the Norwegian coast. There it's supposed to be visibility unlimited. I certainly hope so. Don't want bad weather to keep the Jerries on the ground."

The Squadron Leader paused and glanced at his wrist watch, and then over at the engine filters climbing down out of the bomber.

"Well, I fancy its about time to get on with it, chaps," he said, and tightened the chin strap of his helmet. "In with you. And a good time for all of us. The dinners will be on me when we reach Moscow."

A couple of minutes later the five were aboard the bomber, and the Squadron Leader was running up the engines for a final instrument check. Then he spoke into his inter-com mike and received an all-set okay from each of the other four. That done with, he kicked off the wheel brakes and started to trundle the giant bomber out onto the field and down to the far end of the take-off runway. He had hardly started taxiing, however, when the Operations Officer in his tower blinked the "Stop" signal with his Aldis signal lamp, and a figure was seen to come dashing out the Depot Office. It was the Depot Adjutant, and he held a sheet of yellow paper in his hand. Dave took a look at the yellow sheet waving around in the wind, and swallowed hard. All of a sudden tiny little balls of cold lead were beginning to bounce around in the pit of his stomach. Why he should suddenly experience the strange sensation, he had no idea. However, the sight of the running Depot Adjutant, and the sheet of yellow paper he carried in his hand, seemed to strike him as a very definite reminder that this was not to be any joy flight, but rather, a deadly serious mission to be carried out on the wing.

And a moment or two later, when the Adjutant climbed aboard the bomber that Squadron Leader Freehill had braked to a halt, and came back into the bomb compartment where the Yank and Freddy were parked, the lumps of lead in Dave's stomach began to bounce around more than ever.

"For you, Captain Dawson," the Adjutant said, and held out the yellow sheet of paper. "From the Air Ministry, special code. Afraid for a moment that you'd be off before we could decode it. But here you are, anyway."

Dave took the yellow sheet of paper and held it so that he and Freddy could read it together. It had been sent by Air Vice-Marshal Leman, and its contents were not what you could call very encouraging, considering. It read:

> "Reason to believe mission known, and attempts will be made to prevent accomplishment at all cost.
>
> "Placing you in command, and ordering you to use your own judgment whether to continue. However, second part already enroute, and will attempt to carry on alone if necessary. Train incident undoubtedly small indication of coming events. Flight course perhaps known, so suggest that change be made when in air. All decisions left to you and Farmer. Good luck, regardless of what you decide to do."

Dawson read the decoded message through twice, and then looked quietly at Freddy Farmer. The English-born youth returned his look, and there was the glint of grim determination in his eyes. Dave grinned, and nodded.

"Just what I'm thinking, too, pal," he grunted.

"What do you mean?" Freddy wanted to know.

Dave tapped the sheet of yellow paper, and shrugged.

"Mighty nice of him to give us an out, if we wanted one," he said. "But we don't. We still want to see Moscow, huh?"

"Very much," Freddy grinned back at him. "Fact is, I'd be delighted to let the blasted Nazi lads try and stop us. We'll carry on just as the second part is doing."

Dave nodded complete agreement. Of course, the "second part" referred to Agent Jones' trip to Urbakh via the southern route. Jones had left already, and if he didn't contact Dave and Freddy at Urbakh he would attempt to reach Tobolsk by hook or by crook on his own. However, Dawson and Farmer had no intention of letting Agent Jones be forced to do that.

"Check and double check," Dave grunted, and handed the yellow sheet to Squadron Leader Freehill, who had come aft from the pilot's compartment.

The senior officer read the message, looked very unhappy for a moment, and then smiled slightly at Dawson.

"A pleasure to take orders from you, old chap," he said easily. "But what are they? Do we go, or do we stay?"

Vickers Wellington bombers

"We go," Dave said quietly. "And the sooner the better."

"Right you are, Skipper!" Freehill said happily. Then with a faint frown, "But the course?"

Dawson opened his mouth to speak, but on second thought checked the words about to come out of it.

"I'll give you the new course as soon as we are in the air," he said. Then turning to the Adjutant, he said with a grin, "Thanks for delivering the message. Will you please communicate to the Air Ministry that we are continuing as originally planned, but will make changes in the flight course?"

"Quite, of course," the Adjutant replied, and turned toward the belly door. "Good luck, chaps."

As soon as the Adjutant was clear of the plane, Squadron Leader Freehill went forward and got the Wellington into motion again. Dave went forward with him and dropped into the co-pilot's seat. Neither spoke a word until the bomber was clear of the ground and prop-clawing up through the dirty grey fog. At five thousand it came out into a tunnel of clear air between two layers of overcast. There Freehill leveled off, pointed his aircraft in a general easterly direction, and turned in the seat to look at Dave.

"Well, what's the decision on the course, Skipper?" he asked. "Better let Parsons know as soon as possible, so he can begin plotting for us."

Dave looked across at him and grinned.

"There's no new course, Squadron Leader," he replied. "Hop her along just as you'd planned."

The other's eyes popped a little, and his jaw sagged in befuddled amazement.

"I say, did I hear you?" he echoed. "The original course? But that message from Air Vice-Marshal Leman said that that course might be known. And—"

"And I hope it is, frankly," Dave replied. "It always throws the Nazis out of step when you do *exactly* what they expect you to do."

"Oh yes, quite," the bomber's pilot grunted with a frown. "But I'm afraid, old chap, that I don't quite follow you."

"Well, it's like this," Dave said, and made a little gesture with one hand. "Of course you can guess by now that Farmer and I are on a little business that would, and does, interest the Nazis plenty. They want us to stay home, but we're not going to. Anyway, in this cockeyed war you can look for enemy agents any place, and usually find them. By that, I mean that ten to one Nazi agents back at Aberdeen know darn well I got a message from Air Vice-Marshal Leman. And ten to one they know what was *in* the message. So, from Leman's warning and suggestion, they are bound to figure that we'll fly a different course. So we just fool them, and don't."

"Good grief!" the Squadron Leader gulped. "You mean, of course, they knew of our original flight course?"

"I don't know for sure, naturally," Dave replied with a shrug. "I'm just playing it that way. And besides—"

"Besides, what?" the Squadron Leader prompted when Dave didn't continue.

"I don't like the weather six hundred miles from the Pole," Dawson said with a grin. "Also, you fellows are counting on a little Jerry plane action. Farmer and I wouldn't want to cheat you out of your fun. Nor would we want to cheat ourselves out of it."

The Squadron Leader beamed silently for a moment. Then he gave a little shake of his head, and an emphatic grunt.

"I don't know a thing about your mission, Dawson," he said. "But there is one thing I *do* know. And definitely so!"

"Which would be?" Dawson echoed.

"That you'll accomplish whatever it is," the other replied firmly. "And with flying colors. You two are just the type. And your past record jolly well proves it, too!"

"Thanks," Dave said quietly. And silently wished that at the moment he felt equally as confident of success.

CHAPTER ELEVEN
MOSCOW MAGIC

Freddy Farmer heaved a long sigh, and shifted, around a little so that he could glance out the bomb compartment window. But what he saw was exactly the same picture he had seen ten minutes before. In fact, it was the same picture he had been looking at for the last two hours or more. Nothing but mass upon mass of dirty grey clouds through which the Wellington bomber prop-clawed, as though it could go on forever, and still there'd be clouds.

"Great grief!" the English youth suddenly groaned. "I've seen enough clouds to last me for the whole war. And two or three other wars, for that matter."

"You and me both!" Dave Dawson grunted, and squinted out the little window on his side. "Talk about your blind flying! This sure isn't any fun for Squadron Leader Freehill, and Navigator Parsons, up front. I'm glad I'm a passenger on this trip."

"Not me!" Freddy said with a shake of his head. "I'd much rather be doing something, instead of just looking at this stuff. However, I suppose we shouldn't complain. With this soup all around, any Jerry planes on the prowl are bound to miss us."

"Unless they should happen to plow into us head on!" retorted Dawson with a grin. "I guess Freehill isn't very happy. He probably figures, by now, that we're bad luck. He was counting on a brush or two with Jerry planes. If this stuff holds all the way to Moscow, he'll have all he can do to find the field and get us down okay. He—What's on your mind, pal?"

Dawson checked himself, and then spoke the last because Freddy Farmer had suddenly stiffened, and pressed his nose against the glass of the compartment window. For a full thirty seconds the English-born air ace acted as though he hadn't heard. Then he turned from the window and made a face.

"Just my imagination going a little haywire from it all, I fancy," he said. "Thought for a moment there I'd spotted Messerschmitt wings through a break in the stuff. But it must have been shadows. It wasn't there the second look I took. Well, I wonder just where we are, and how far from Moscow?"

Dawson glanced at his wrist watch and shrugged.

"Another hour at least, I guess," he said. "Longer, if we've run into head winds. Let's go forward and find out from Freehill."

"You go," Freddy Farmer suggested with a yawn. "I'm quite comfortable, thanks, though terribly bored. Find out all the details, my good fellow, and then report back to me. There's a good chap."

"And who was your valet last year?" Dawson growled, and got up onto his feet. "Nuts, I'll report back to you! You can just stay sprawled out there, and wonder."

"Sorry, old thing," Freddy Farmer grinned after him, "but I can't be bothered doing even that. Let me know, anyway, when we arrive at Moscow. I wonder if Stalin will be there at the airport to meet me?"

"He won't!" Dawson snapped, and started forward. "Stalin has sense!"

Leaving Freddy to mull that one over, Dawson made his way along the catwalk to the navigator's compartment. Flight Lieutenant Parsons was bent scowling over his chart table, so Dave didn't pause to ask questions. He continued on by and finally slipped into the co-pilot's seat. Squadron Leader Freehill glanced over at him and grinned sadly.

"Looks like a bit of a washout for our hopes, what?" the pilot murmured, and let go of the controls long enough to wave a hand at the walls of cloud that pressed in from all sides. "Don't mind, do you, if we finally sit down in Iceland, or some place like that? Old Parsons is about ready to cut his throat. Mostly instrument and dead reckoning now. We don't dare open the radio and ask for a bearing. The Russians probably wouldn't give it to us, anyway. It would reveal their station locations, too. Well, we've got plenty of gas, anyway."

"Now I'm all cheered up," Dawson replied with a grin. "I had thought that maybe you had no idea where you were."

"Oh, perish the thought!" the other said with a chuckle, and pointed a finger downward. "Always know where I am. The ground is that way, straight down eighteen thousand! But don't ask me who owns that particular bit of it. Blast this stuff, though! When in the world are we coming out of it?"

Dawson only half heard the last. What he took to be slight movement off to his left had suddenly caught and held his attention. He stared hard at the spot, but for all of his effort he could see nothing but dirty grey clouds. True, they were a bit lighter in spots: an indication that the sun was doing its best to burn a path through. But the stuff was still too thick for the sun's efforts to make more than a faint glow here and there. However, just as Dave was about to turn his head and look at Squadron Leader Freehill, he caught a glimpse of movement again. And this time he saw something that brought him up straight in the seat, and started his heart to hammering against his ribs.

Just off the right wing, and no more than a hundred feet below, half of a German Messerschmitt wing had cut out into clear air, and instantly

Messershmitt 110

cut back in out of sight again. But he had seen the square-tipped wing, clearly. And he had also seen the black cross outlined in white. So Freddy Farmer's imagination hadn't been going haywire! There was a Jerry ship up there in the air with them! But for what reason? Was the Jerry lost, and milling around trying to find his way home? Or was he playing cat and mouse with the Wellington, and keeping tabs on its flight almost due eastward?

Dave asked himself the question, but he didn't bother guessing around at the answer. Instead, he kept his eyes on the spot where he had seen the Messerschmitt wing, and reached out with his near hand to rap Freehill on the arm.

"We've got company, sir!" he called out. "Just saw a hunk of Messerschmitt One-Ten wing cut up into clear air off to starboard and down a hundred feet."

"Really?" came the excited answer. "Do you think he spotted us? Could be one, you know. Parsons figures that we're about over the middle of Occupied Latvia. Just one, eh?"

"Just one, I saw," Dawson replied, and continued to bore the dirty grey clouds with his eyes. "Maybe he's some lost Nazi tramp, or maybe he's up here on purpose looking for us. How about buzzing Sergeant Dilling to spin his wave length dial? Maybe he'll pick up that bird talking to ground stations—or some of his pals in the air with him."

"Splendid idea!" Squadron Leader Freehill said instantly. "I'll do that. Stand by, half a moment, and keep your eyes skinned."

Dawson heard Freehill mumbling words over the inter-com to the Wellington's radioman, but he didn't bother straining his ears to catch each word. He kept his head turned to the right, and his eyes roaming about the masses of dirty grey clouds. Perhaps four minutes dragged by, and then suddenly he felt Squadron Leader Freehill's hand on his left shoulder.

"Top-hole idea, that!" the British bomber pilot shouted. "Just got a reply buzz from Dilling. He picked up a little something. Seems the beggar is up here tailing us, and keeping the ground informed. That means there must be clear air soon, and the beggars will be there to meet us. Splendid, I say! They'll wish they hadn't, I fancy!"

Dawson grinned, stiff-lipped, but didn't say anything for a moment, or two. It wasn't that he didn't welcome a scrap with Nazi planes. Well, not exactly. The point was that Freddy and he didn't have time right now to mill around the sky with Nazi pilots. This wasn't a patrol with a chip on his shoulder. This was an emergency flight to Moscow, and the sooner they got there the better it would be. No, a mess of Nazi Messerschmitts suddenly blocking the way wouldn't be a diversion that he would exactly welcome now. Freddy and he had a mission to carry out, and to get shot down, and be forced to bail out over enemy-occupied territory, would of course knock the whole carefully worked out plan high, wide and handsome. No! To be truthful, he wanted very much *not* to meet any German planes this trip. For once he had no desire to give battle to Hitler's black-winged vultures. He wanted only to arrive safely in Moscow, and as quickly as this Wellington bomber could get him there. However, if—

He had automatically slipped on the co-pilot's inter-com head phones, so at that moment he heard Freddy Farmer's sharp, clear voice.

"A Jerry One-Ten dead astern of us, Squadron Leader!" Freddy reported. "I'm at the tail gun now. The blighter knows we're here. Shall I open fire?"

Freehill glanced over at Dawson and caught the Yank's quick nod and grin.

"Blast the beggar, of course!" he called back. "Shoot the Iron Cross right off his tunic, old thing. And—"

And that was all Squadron Leader Freehill said for the moment. He cut himself off short, and for a very good reason. The wall of dirty grey cloud suddenly ended as clean as a whistle. The Wellington went zooming out into a world of brilliant sunshine—and considerably more than that. To Dave, snapping his eyes forward, it seemed as though half the German Luftwaffe were milling around in the air directly ahead. He took one swift glance at the aerial picture, and then jerked off his intercom phones, tore out of the co-pilot's seat, and went charging back to the blister gun turret amidships.

By the time he had reached the blister and was swinging his twin guns into position, the air all around was alive with German planes, and the entire heavens shook and vibrated with the savage snarl and yammer of aerial machine guns, plus the louder, deeper note of aerial cannon fire.

As though Lady Luck had simply been waiting for Dawson to swing into action, the square-cut wings of a One-Ten came smack into his sights. Instantly he jabbed the electric trigger button, and the One-Ten just as promptly acted as though it had suddenly flown right into a brick wall. Both its wings came off as though sliced by a knife. The fuselage rolled over twice, and like a crazy rocket went zooming upward to smash square into a second One-Ten banking off to the side. A burst of flame followed the mid air crash, and the whole blazing mass went slithering down out of sight, leaving behind a long trail of oily black smoke.

The instant the mid-air crash took place, Dawson whipped his eyes off it and swung his guns to bear on a third One-Ten. Before he could press the trigger, though, he heard Freddy Farmer's guns in the tail start snarling. And the Messerschmitt simply wasn't there any more. It was just a shower of pieces falling downward through the golden sunshine.

No cheer of joy broke from Dawson's throat, though. There were three One-Tens down, and maybe a couple of others that Freehill and Sergeant Dilling and Flight Lieutenant Parsons had nailed. But there were still ten times that number of German planes still twisting and boring in, and raking the Wellington from spinning props to rudder post with their furious fire. Dawson wasn't sure, but he thought he could feel the bomber shake and tremble as each new burst of bullets tore into it.

He didn't bother to look around, though, for any signs of damage. He was too busy holding up his end of the terribly uneven fight, smacking and slapping away at anything winged that came into his sights, and silently damning the invention known as the aircraft detector. The aircraft detector, of course, explained the presence of all those German planes. The Nazis, if Air Vice-Marshal Leman's wire was to be believed, knew that the Wellington would be heading for Moscow. Maybe they hadn't known the route to be flown in advance. But they didn't have to know it. Aircraft detectors all up and down the German-occupied coast of Europe would have been constantly on the alert. Any aircraft heard that could not be identified as Nazi would have been investigated instantly, of course.

That explained that lone Messerschmitt flirting about with the Wellington in the clouds. Its pilot had spotted them, judged their course, and communicated with ground stations. And—and there were the aerial butchers waiting for the Wellington the instant it came prop-clawing out into clear air.

"So if you want it this way, then okay!" Dawson roared impulsively, and let fly at a brace of One-Tens cutting around to catch the bomber in a cold meat cross-fire.

Perhaps, if they had been given a few seconds more, the Nazis would have succeeded in their goal. But Dawson's deadly fire put an end to the attempt, and a very speedy end, too. A two second burst caught the One-Ten on the left square in the cockpit. The pilot died instantly, and so he couldn't control the One-Ten from veering off drunkenly to the other side. Too late the other Messerschmitt pilot saw what was headed his way. True, he made a very good try, but it wasn't any better than no try at all. The One-Ten with a dead pilot at the controls whanged up into his belly, and speared him like a fish. Seconds later there was just a great big ball of seething flame flip-flopping down into oblivion.

"Seems to be the day for Nazis ramming into each other!" Dave gasped out, and swung his guns for a new target. "Well, that's—Hey! Well, what do you know? Hey, *everybody!* See what we've got to help us. Boy, oh boy!"

Dawson wildly shouted other things, but in his great joy he didn't even know what he said. All he was conscious of was the very delightful fact that there were other besides German wings in the air about the Wellington. There were planes with the Red Star of the Soviet Air Force on the wings and fuselage. They were the swift and deadly Russian "Rata" One-Sixteen B pursuit aircraft, powered by special 1,000 hp. M-Sixty-Three engines of Wright "Cyclone" design. Out of the sun they had come like

a downed Rata, otherwise known as the Polikarpov I-16

so many crazed hornets on the rampage. And even as Dave saw them, four German Messerschmitts simply broke apart in the air and fell away out of sight.

It was one of the most perfectly executed aerial attacks Dawson had ever witnessed. Each Russian pilot seemed to know just which Messerschmitt he was to handle. And he went right smack at his victim and did the job with the least amount of bullets possible. In fact, the arrival of those Soviet Ratas was almost as though invisible hands had swept an invisible broom across the skies, and taken three fourths of the German Messerschmitts along with it. The other fourth that was missed by the invisible broom didn't hang around for a second sweeping. Every Luftwaffe pilot dropped the nose of his plane, and got out of there as fast as his screaming engine could take him. A flight or so of the Ratas gave chase, just to keep the Messerschmitts on their way, while the other Rata pilots took up close escort position on all four sides of the Wellington, and above it.

A little over half an hour later Squadron Leader Freehill sat the bullet-riddled Wellington down at the Moscow airport as lightly as a feather floating on a strip of velvet. A few of the Ratas landed alongside, and the aerial cavalcade taxied over to the huge camouflaged hangars. Both Dawson and Freddy Farmer were up front with Freehill by then, and they all saw the small group of high Soviet military officials who were waiting for the Wellington to taxi in.

"Either of you chaps the President of the U.S. in disguise?" the Squadron Leader asked with a chuckle. "Quite a reception committee here to greet you. That tall, dark chap on the left is none other than Colonel General Vladimir, in case you don't know."

"I didn't," Dave grunted.

"Nor did I," Freddy Farmer echoed.

"Well, as the Yanks would put it," the Squadron Leader said, "Stalin and Vladimir are the two chaps who really make the Soviet tick. Vladimir has more titles, and is in charge of more things, than you could shake a stick at. That he is here to meet you two chaps must mean that you are very important lads in this war business."

"That lets me out," Dawson grinned. "Of course, maybe the Russians have suddenly decided to learn to drink tea, and that's why Farmer is making this trip. I wouldn't know. My job is simply to trail him around and see that he doesn't get into trouble. You know, international complications?"

"Rot!" Freddy snorted. "Why not tell the Squadron Leader the truth? Tell him that the Russians are simply anxious to see a crazy, balmy Yank who somehow manages to keep on missing Nazi bullets. And that I'm along to prevent the Russians from putting you in a museum!"

"Well, I was wondering about your secret," Freehill laughed. "Now I know, definitely. Anyway, I fancy we'll be parting company soon. But all kind of luck, chaps. And if you happen to be going back by this way, I wish you'd let me know. I'll put in the request to pilot the return trip. Didn't get half the Jerries we could have, if the Russian chaps hadn't shown up, you know. Maybe we can do better next time, what?"

"Well, we can try," Dawson said absently, and stared at the group of Russian officials who were now walking out toward the taxiing bomber.

"Yes, quite!" Freddy Farmer also murmured absently. "A very nice bomber team we make. Quite!"

CHAPTER TWELVE
THE LIVING DEAD

The Russian Staff car reminded Dawson of a Ford. As a matter of fact, he was pretty sure that it was a Yank Ford made under license in a Soviet factory. However, he didn't let his thoughts dwell on the car too long. For one thing, the uniformed driver seemed to be attempting to smash every existing speed record. And for another thing, the instant Freddy and he had climbed down out of the Wellington things had happened like exploding firecrackers.

Colonel General Vladimir had stepped forward, introduced himself, and greeted them warmly. Then almost before they could return the greeting, the Russian had steered them right by the other officials and into the Russian-made Ford. At a word from the Colonel General, the uniformed chauffeur had shifted gears, and away they had gone.

At first, Dawson hadn't minded these strange actions very much because the car roared through the heart of Moscow and he was able to get his first view of the Kremlin, and Red Square. But that had been half an hour previously, and by now the car was approaching empty country that held no interest or attraction for him. And so he began to wonder in earnest why this sudden mysterious move, and also why the Colonel General, seated between Freddy and him on the back seat, was content to stare out through the windshield in stony silence.

Suddenly, though, as the car spun around the corner of some woods and onto a long straight road, the Russian official seemed to let go a little sigh of relief, and relaxed slightly. He barked an order in his native tongue to the driver, and immediately the speed of the car was reduced by a good third. The Colonel General looked at Dave and Freddy each in turn, and smiled pleasantly.

"Your heads are crammed full of questions?" he said with a chuckle. "Is it not so?"

"Well, I was wondering just where the fire was," Dawson replied. "I mean, of course, why all the hurry?"

"Yes, quite," Freddy Farmer murmured. "Has something unexpected happened, Colonel General?"

"That is the reason for the haste," the Russian replied with a little gesture. "So that the unexpected would *not* happen, you see? In the Soviet we do not take unnecessary chances. It is stupid to do such things. So when you arrive we do not give ears the chance to hear much, or eyes the chance to see much. I would swear that there is not one Gestapo secret agent in all of Moscow, but I am not content with just *believing* so. All men can be wrong. So I take no chances, in case I am wrong. This mission you are on means much to Russia. There is no telling how much it will mean. So it is only natural that we do all in our power to give you the aid you need, and to protect you as long as we can. Your pardon one moment, please."

The Colonel General leaned forward and rapped out some obvious orders to the driver. The man at the wheel nodded his head to show that he had heard and understood. Then the Russian sat back on the seat again, and addressed himself to the two boys.

"Tomorrow, I am afraid," he said, with an odd little half-smile, "there will be harsh things said about Russia by her allies. Your England and your United States will not be pleased to learn that you two died while under our care."

"Huh?" Dawson gulped out as the other paused, and seemed waiting. "I mean, what did you say, Colonel General? Something about Farmer and me getting killed?"

"Exactly," the other nodded with the odd little smile still on his lips. "Burned alive in an automobile wreck. Fortunately, though, I will manage to escape with my life. I will be most brokenhearted when I give out the statement to the representatives of the Foreign Press in Moscow. And there will be an expression of deep sorrow from Premier Joseph Stalin, too. It will, indeed, be a sad affair, that meeting with the press tomorrow."

The Russian lapsed into sudden silence again, and Dawson wasn't sure whether he should take it just as a cockeyed dream, or jump out of the car in case the world had actually gone upside down all of a sudden. He did neither, of course. Instead he shot a quick hard side glance at the Russian, and caught the faint grin that tugged at the corners of the officer's mouth. Then he found himself looking straight into a pair of twinkling black eyes.

"I am what you call in America a mad Russian, eh, Captain Dawson," the Colonel General suddenly boomed out. "Forgive me, but it is like me to say strange things and watch people's faces. However, it is a little true. You and your gallant comrade are to die in a burning automobile wreck. That is, as far as the rest of the world is concerned. It is like this. Our enemies know more about this mission of yours than we would like them to know. Twice they have done what they could to remove you and your friend, Captain Farmer. Oh, yes. I know about that train affair in Scotland. Since then Air Vice-Marshal Leman has communicated with Soviet Intelligence. And your recent air battle was no accident, either."

"And but for the very welcome arrival of your planes, it might have ended the wrong way, too!" Dave spoke up quickly.

Colonel General Vladimir nodded, and beamed his thanks.

"A compliment twice over, coming from a war pilot of your record, Captain Dawson," he said gravely. "Ah, yes! Once many people laughed at the mention of Soviet planes, and Soviet pilots. But they are not laughing any more. Particularly the Nazi Luftwaffe. But, as I was saying, twice the Nazis have tried to remove you, and have failed. They know that you have reached Moscow. Your next destination perhaps they know, and perhaps they don't. However, we will attempt to cause them to lose interest in you both. Lose interest because they believe you are both dead. The results of crude Soviet bungling, they will no doubt scream over their propaganda radios. But let them! It does not matter if it all helps you to complete your delicate mission successfully."

The Russian paused, nodded for emphasis, and lapsed into silence again. Freddy Farmer didn't like that, and did something about it.

"Just how are you to arrange for us to burn up in a car wreck, Colonel General?" he asked bluntly.

The Russian shrugged, and gestured with both of his hands, palms upward.

"That will be very simple," he said. Then, nodding ahead, he continued, "In a few moments, now. Just around that turn you see up ahead. There will be a car waiting for us, just off the road. You will change to it, and this one will be driven into a tree so that it will be suitably wrecked, and then touched off with a match. This driver will then continue on with you in the hidden car, and leave me to explain things to the first car that passes by."

"I see," Dawson grunted after a moment's thought. "Three of us to burn up, eh? But what about three fire-charred bodies in the wreckage, so there'll be sure to be no questions asked?"

"Also simple," the Russian replied in a grim voice. "Three Nazis will take your places. Three dead ones. They were shot yesterday. They served their mad Fuehrer in life, so they will serve our cause in death. Well, we approach the point where we part for a few hours. I will see you again tomorrow, or the next day."

"Next day?" Dawson echoed sharply. "Where? What do you mean by that remark, Colonel General?"

"For two days it is best for you to remain dead, and safely hidden," the Russian officer explained. "The English Agent Jones has not yet completed even a third of his long journey. It is best for you all to arrive at Urbakh the same day. To arrive ahead of him, and be forced to wait around for his arrival, might not be good. So you will rest for a few days in our care. I do not think that you will find it too unpleasant. Well, we are almost there."

There were a whole lot more questions that Dave wanted to ask, but the Colonel General sort of gave the impression that the question period was over. Besides, the car was cutting around the turn in the road and slowing down toward a full stop. So Dave held his tongue, and left his questions hanging in his brain. He looked ahead but did not see any second car. That is, for a moment or two he didn't see one. But suddenly, as the Russian Ford came abreast of a narrow dirt road leading off through the woods, there he spotted the second car pulled well up under the trees.

When their car came to a final halt, the Colonel General was out of it in a flash and turning around to smile and motion for them to follow.

"Come with me," he said. "He will take care of everything. He used to smash cars for a living before the war, like the dare-devils in your Hollywood. It will be amusing to watch him."

It wasn't particularly amusing to Dawson and Farmer so much as it was fascinatingly gruesome. The Russian chauffeur hauled three dead Nazis out of the car hidden under the trees and placed two of them in the rear seat of the Ford. The third he wedged in behind the wheel. Then, squeezing in on top of the dead German, he got the Ford tearing along at high speed down the road. The instant the car was going full out he gave the wheel a sharp twist, and seemed virtually to shoot his body up out from behind the wheel. He landed lightly on his feet on the road like a highly trained acrobat, and the Russian Ford went tearing at terrific speed straight into a couple of giant tree trunks.

Colonel General Vladimir said that they were to touch a match to the wreck, but a single split second after the Ford struck the tree trunks it became instantly evident that no match would be needed. A great glob of smoke belched up from under the crumpled engine hood, and was followed by a tongue of hissing orange-red flame. And by the time Dawson could blink the car was completely enveloped in flame.

"And so that is finished," he suddenly heard the Colonel General break through his thoughts. "Now, into this car, please. There is no time to loiter here. You must be on your way. A pleasant journey, Captains. And we will meet again tomorrow, or the next day. Do not be alarmed. I would trust him as I would trust my own son—if I had but been blessed with one."

Even as the Russian talked he guided Dawson and Freddy Farmer into the rear seat of the half hidden car, and then stepped back to allow the driver to get in behind the wheel. And no sooner had the driver settled himself than he kicked the engine into life, shifted gears, and started off. Both Dawson and Farmer glanced back at the Colonel General, but the Russian seemed no longer aware of their existence. He was busy tearing shreds of cloth from his uniform, and smearing rich Russian soil on his face and hands. And then he faded from view around a bend in the wooded road. Dawson turned to the side and looked into Freddy Farmer's saucer-sized eyes.

"Sweet tripe!" he grunted. "In this neck of the woods they sure do things fast, and let you find out later, don't they?"

"Not half, they don't!" Freddy exclaimed with a bewildered shake of his head. "Well, love a duck! What a bloke that Colonel General is! Why, I hadn't half begun to ask questions. Where in the world is he going to hide us out, I'd like to know?"

"Me, too!" Dawson said with a grim nod, and leaned toward the driver's seat. "Where are we headed, driver?" he called out.

The Russian chauffeur slowed up a little and turned to give them a blank smile and a blanker look. Then he seemed to guess the meaning of Dawson's question, and opened and shut the fingers of one upraised hand three times. Then he smiled and nodded and returned his attention to driving. Dawson made sounds in his throat and sank back on the seat.

"And that helps a lot, I don't think!" he growled. "No speak our lingo. But I guess he guessed the question, and was telling us we'll get there in fifteen minutes, or fifteen hours, or maybe fifteen years. But there's nothing we can do about it, anyway. And how do you like being a dead man, pal?"

The English youth glanced up at the sky that seemed to hold the hint of coming winter, and shuddered slightly.

"In this country I don't fancy it a bit," he said. "Not even a little bit. But it is a clever trick by the Russians. And I wish I could hear the Nazi propaganda chaps scream about it over the radio. It'll almost make us famous, you know."

"I'll take vanilla, thank you!" Dawson grunted, and stared at the winding road ahead. "After, and if, we finish this job, I hope I can get a few days off to really see Moscow, and these parts around here. But right now I want to keep going, and get the darn thing cleaned up. Two days, he said? Not so good. A lot of things can happen in two days."

"Well, as you said, there's nothing we can do about it," Freddy Farmer said with a shrug. "So that's that. Just the same, I'd like to know what that chauffeur chap meant by his crazy hand signals."

Dawson didn't bother trying to answer that question, and Freddy Farmer didn't bother to repeat it. Both youths simply lapsed into brooding silence, and absently stared at the winding road that seemed to go on winding forever through endless woods. However, at the end of ten minutes they came out of the woods and onto a road leading to a small peasant village. And at the end of exactly fifteen minutes from the time of the chauffeur's finger signals, the car was halted in front of a rough two-story wooden house. The chauffeur got out, bowed to them, and motioned for them to get out too. They did, and followed him up the three steps to the front door of the house.

The chauffeur knocked on the door, and he had no more than taken his knuckles away than it was opened and they saw a uniformed figure just inside the doorway. The chauffeur saluted smartly, rattled something off in his native tongue, and then hurried past Dawson and Farmer, and down the steps to the car. In less than nothing flat he had the car rolling at a fast clip off up the village street. Dave and Freddy glanced at each other and mutually wondered, what next?

They didn't have to wait long. The dimly outlined uniformed figure just inside the doorway spoke to them in a low, rich voice.

"Come in, please, Captains Dawson and Farmer. I am happy that you have arrived safely in Russia. And I am honored to be able to share with you the adventures that lie ahead. Come in, please."

A crazy conglomeration of mixed thoughts and emotions raced through Dawson as he stepped through the door and into a very shadowy hallway. Freddy Farmer followed right at his heels, and the sudden change of light threw the eyes of both out of focus for a few seconds. But when they were able to see clearly again, they found themselves looking at a very young and very good-looking Russian Senior Lieutenant of Intelligence.

Yet very good-looking was not quite correct. Very pretty would have been a little better, because, like bombs exploding in their heads, they both realized in the same instant that the Senior Lieutenant was a *girl* of just about their own age! That bit of truth just about topped off all of the high speed action they'd witnessed since arriving in Russia, and for a long minute both were too stunned to do anything but salute smartly and just stand there practically gaping at the girl. She glanced from one to the other, then gave a little low laugh.

"So you are surprised, eh?" she echoed. "Well, there are a lot of women like me fighting for Russia. But let me introduce myself. I am Senior Lieutenant Nasha Petrovski, of Soviet Intelligence. Until Colonel General Vladimir says it is time to leave for Urbakh, you are honored guests of my mother and myself. And later we will be comrades in arms for a great and worthy cause. But I keep you standing here while I chatter. Come and meet my mother. And then I will show you to the room that has been made ready for you. This way, please, Captains."

And like a couple of dumbfounded wooden Indians, Dave Dawson and Freddy Farmer followed her into the ground floor parlor.

CHAPTER THIRTEEN
HIGH STAKES

The sound was akin to that of an invisible giant of the sky tearing off a section of a tin roof with his bare hands. It began high up in the black night sky, and grew louder and louder until it seemed that their eardrums had been driven clear back into their brains. And then suddenly it turned into a gigantic explosion that made the very earth lurch and shudder, and seemed to stop spinning for a moment and go staggering across limitless space.

"If there was only a night fighter handy! Boy! What I wouldn't give for a night fighter right now!"

Dave Dawson muttered out the words aloud, hardly conscious that he had spoken them. With Freddy Farmer, and Senior Lieutenant Nasha Petrovski, he was standing out in the back yard of the Russian girl's home, and staring up at a sneak night raid by Nazi bombers on Moscow a dozen or so miles away. It was only a nuisance raid, and Soviet anti-aircraft guns and Soviet night fighters were making the Luftwaffe pay a heavy price for the few Moscow buildings they hit with their bombs.

However, though the Nazis were unable to hit anything, that fact did not curb Dawson's desire to be up there in the searchlight-laced sky, dealing out his share of trouble and doom to the raiding vultures. And, incidentally, complete inactivity for three days and nights added greatly to his desire to be aloft in all the fuss. And so it was only natural that such an expression should slip off his lips automatically.

"That is the way all good soldiers should feel, Captain Dawson," he suddenly heard the Russian girl's voice at his side. "To do nothing, when there is so much to be done, hurts more than the wounds of battle. I know just how you feel, yes. And I sympathize with you. Time never waits."

"You've got something there, Senior Lieutenant," Dave said, taking his eyes off the sky battle to look at her. "And I've been wondering. Do you think Colonel General Vladimir has forgotten about us? Or maybe that something has happened to him? It's been *three* days now."

"Quite," Freddy Farmer joined in the conversation. "He said he expected to join us the very next day. But we haven't even heard a word. Or have you, Senior Lieutenant?"

The Russian Intelligence agent shook her head, and made a faint gesture.

"To me there has come no word," she said slowly, as though selecting each English spoken word. "But I do not worry. The Colonel General never forgets anything. And nothing will ever happen to the Colonel

General but good things. If it were to be different, the bad things would have happened long before this time. Like you I wait, and I am restless to be in action again. But I do not worry. When it is the right time, the Colonel General will arrive."

Dave considered that in silence for a couple of minutes and watched the sky battle move across the heavens farther and farther to the southwest. The Nazis had dumped their eggs hastily and were trying to scurry back home, but the Red Air Force was chopping down not a few of them en route. Over toward Moscow there were the crimson glows of half a dozen fires. But even as Dave stared at them the glows grew fainter and fainter, indicating that the city's fire fighters were quickly getting the flames under control. The "flak" fire had died out almost entirely, and the only sounds to be heard were the muffled roar of distant aircraft engines, punctuated now and then by the short, stabbing chatter of Red night fighter machine guns.

"Well, that's that," Dave finally spoke again. "The Berlin newspapers will probably scream tomorrow that there isn't anything left of Moscow. But Uncle Goering will know different when he gets the raiding reports. And maybe he'll worry another ten pounds off his bay window."

"But he'll no doubt put it right back on as soon as he has breakfast," Freddy Farmer grunted. "And speaking of food—Oh, so sorry, Senior Lieutenant. I beg your pardon."

"For what?" the Russian girl asked with a flashing smile, and a teasing lilt to her voice. "Because you speak the truth?"

"But I say, really!" the English youth stammered, and his face went beet red in the darkness. "I didn't think, you know. And it was most impolite. I—"

"Stop making pretty speeches!" Dawson ribbed him. "Be yourself, and truthful. I'll try to apologize to the Senior Lieutenant for you. You see, Senior Lieutenant, my friend has a hollow leg, so no matter how much he eats he never can seem to get enough. Confidentially, the British Air Ministry seriously considered dumping him off in Occupied France for a spell so that he could get used to going without food. But I put in a plea for him, and—"

"And why should not one of England's heroes eat, if he likes?" Senior Lieutenant Nasha Petrovski demanded quietly. "But of course! Come, Captain Farmer. Let us return inside the house. My mother will find us a good meal, have no fear."

"Your slave, Senior Lieutenant," Freddy said, and bowed low. Then turning to Dave, he said, "You may remain here on guard, Captain

Dawson. And you might hunt around for a bit of anti-aircraft shrapnel that I could keep as a souvenir. After you, Senior Lieutenant."

"But no, no!" the Russian girl exclaimed with a laugh. "No doubt Captain Dawson is hungry, too. And is he not also one of England's heroes?"

"A debatable question, Senior Lieutenant," Freddy Farmer said quickly with a shrug. "But, if you insist. And to tell the truth, he is afraid of the dark, you know. Very well, Captain Dawson, you may join us."

"And I'll—!" Dave growled, but instantly checked his words, and the quick step he took toward his pal.

All three of them laughed as though there were no such thing as a war existing, and went trooping back into the house. Madam Petrovski had turned on the lights, and had also anticipated their wishes, for the table was set, and three bowls of energy-building hot soup were waiting for them. As Dave looked at her aged, wrinkled face, and the black eyes that glowed with the undying faith and determination of Russia, herself, a warm glow closed about his heart, and a polite and sincere compliment rose to his lips.

But he never spoke that compliment, for at that moment a car braked to a stop outside, and almost instantly there came the sound of feet on the front steps, and that of knuckles rapping sharply on the front door. And before Dawson could so much as blink, Senior Lieutenant Nasha Petrovski had glided out of the room, and opened the door. Split seconds later Colonel General Vladimir came striding into the room. Dave and Freddy sprang to attention and saluted. The Colonel General first bowed and saluted Madam Petrovski, and then he returned their salute.

"Good evening, Captains," he said with his odd smile. "You have perhaps been wondering, eh? Well, there have been things to wonder about. Be seated, please, all of you."

As the Colonel General spoke, the old familiar lumps of cold lead began to bounce around in Dawson's stomach. And it wasn't from hunger, either. The Colonel General's eyes were still flashing with inner fire, but in their depths Dawson could catch just the faintest tint of worry and concern. He turned to hold a chair for Madam Petrovski, only to realize that she had left the room, and closed the door. He must have blinked at that, for Senior Lieutenant Petrovski suddenly caught his eye, and smiled.

"It is always like that," she said softly. "My mother prefers to pray, and listen to the story when all has been accomplished."

"But there is no soldier who loves Russia more," the Colonel General spoke up gravely. "Nor one who would sacrifice more for his homeland."

The silence that followed the Russian officer's words seemed to say, "Amen," to that. Then a moment later the Colonel General motioned for them all to sit down, and took a chair for himself.

"There is a decision for us to make," he said bluntly. "A decision forced by bad news. But no! That is not correct. A decision because there has been no news at all."

"Agent Jones!" Dawson breathed softly, as he leaned forward on the edge of his seat. "I've had a feeling!"

Colonel General Vladimir shot him a sharp piercing look, and then nodded.

"You are correct, Captain Dawson," he said, tight-lipped. "No news of Agent Jones since he left Baghdad, in Syria, twenty-four hours ago. His plane was to land at Baku, in the south Caucasus, but it has not arrived."

A profound silence settled over the room as the Colonel General's words died away to the echo. Then Freddy Farmer broke it with a single word question.

"Weather?"

The Russian officer shrugged, and sighed heavily.

"Perhaps," he grunted. "My reports say that it has been very bad in that section for several days. True, he may have been forced down, and will continue as soon as weather permits. But—but it is also possible that other things may have happened to his pilot and plane. Who is there to tell? Our enemies have ears and eyes, as we all well know. They also have guns, and know how to use them. So the truth may be one of many answers."

"So what?" Dave murmured. Then, quickly catching himself, "I beg your pardon, sir. I mean, what is the decision to be made?"

The Russian looked at him, and Dawson had the sudden funny feeling that the man was looking straight down into his heart.

"You cannot guess, Captain Dawson?" he suddenly asked softly.

Dave looked blank for a moment, and then felt the rush of hot blood to his face.

"Yes, sir," he replied as soon as he could. "I think we should decide to carry on with our end of it, Agent Jones or no Agent Jones. Somebody's got to get to Tobolsk and find Ivan Nikolsk. So we're elected."

"Ah! The words of a gallant soldier that all Russia must admire!"

It was Senior Lieutenant Petrovski who had spoken the words, and Dave could almost feel the blood burst out through the skin of his face. Not for a million dollars would he have dared glance at the expression that must have been in Freddy Farmer's eyes. To do so would undoubtedly have meant the end of a beautiful friendship. So he kept his gaze riveted on the Colonel General's face. But there was no glint of merriment in the Russian's eyes, just the flash of fire and grim resolve.

"You speak wise words, Captain Dawson," he said quietly. "The stakes are so high they demand any and every effort. Without this Agent Jones the difficulties are increased six times over. But there is hope. And we must cling to that, always."

The Russian paused a brief moment to nod his head at Senior Lieutenant Nasha Petrovski, seated on the other side of the table.

"The Senior Lieutenant knows every foot of ground in the Tobolsk area," he continued presently. "She is sure she even remembers the old farm where Ivan Nikolsk was last seen. If anybody can find Ivan Nikolsk, it will be the Senior Lieutenant. And when she finds him—"

The Colonel General paused and frowned slightly. The Russian girl seemed instantly to guess what thought was in his mind, for she spoke up quickly.

"And if he will not tell to me, a Russian woman, the secrets that are buried deep in his brain," she said evenly, "then we will bring him to Moscow, to the Kremlin. And then the Russian in him will speak. It will have to be so!"

Dave, looking at the girl, suddenly didn't see a girl at all. He saw a soldier; a fighting soldier of the Soviet, who would not stop at bullets, or shells, or fire and flood to gain through to an objective. Nasha Petrovski was a girl, but hers was the bravery, the courage, and the fighting spirit, to be surpassed by no man's!

"Yes, it will have to be so!" Colonel General Vladimir echoed the words. "And when Ivan Nikolsk speaks we will have only to match in his words with all that Agent Jones has reported to Air Vice-Marshal Leman, which, of course, has been transmitted to me in secret code. Yes! The decision is to go to Urbakh, and if Agent Jones has not arrived, to go on over the enemy positions to Tobolsk, and find this Ivan Nikolsk. That is agreed, eh?"

Dave, Freddy, and the girl Senior Lieutenant simply nodded gravely. There was no need for words.

"Good!" the Colonel General said, and stood up. "So there is no time like this time to begin. Senior Lieutenant Petrovski! Five minutes to say farewell to your mother. Then you will conduct the Captains to the aircraft. I will be waiting for your return to Moscow, and like all Russia, praying my prayers for your safety and success!"

As the Russian officer stopped speaking, the girl sprang to her feet, saluted smartly, and then left the room. The Colonel General waited until the door was closed, and then looked hard at Dawson and Freddy Farmer.

"There is one thing of which I will speak, Captains," he said quietly. "The Senior Lieutenant is a woman, and there are those who do not believe that a woman's place is in the line of enemy fire. But here in the Soviet we are all soldiers of the line, men and women. Their courage is the same, their eyes just as sharp, and their trigger finger just as steady. And have no thoughts about the Senior Lieutenant under fire, or in the face of any danger. She has won her rank the same as any Soviet man soldier. She has won medals for valor, though she does not wear them. So have no worries because she is a woman. Three hundred and six Nazi soldiers have died from a rifle or a machine gun in her hands. Keep that truth in mind. And now I salute you in the name of the Soviet Republics. God's speed, God's courage, and God's blessings be with you from the beginning of your journey to your safe and successful return."

The Colonel General saluted, and by the time Dawson and Freddy were halfway up on their feet, he had whirled and walked out of the room. The two youths checked themselves, and sank back into their chairs. Dave swallowed hard, and whistled softly.

"Suffering catfish!" he gulped. "Three hundred and six Nazi tramps! My gosh! And me thinking *I'd* seen some of this war!"

"Quite!" Freddy Farmer murmured. "Makes a chap feel like he's only been playing at soldiers. But—"

"But what?" Dave grunted. And then as he saw the glint in Freddy Farmer's eyes he wished he had bitten off his tongue, instead.

"But *I'll* be in safe company," the English youth shot at him. "Oh, quite! With *two* gallant soldiers that all Russia must admire!"

Dave's eyes flashed fire, and he started up out of his chair. But he dropped quickly back as he heard the footsteps of Senior Lieutenant Nasha Petrovski returning to the room.

"Remember it always, you bum!" he whispered to Freddy. "That a girl once saved your life, by coming through that door over there!"

CHAPTER FOURTEEN
SUCCESS OR SUICIDE?

Senior Lieutenant Petrovski reached across from the co-pilot's seat to touch Dawson's arm, and then point a finger.

"That black smudge ahead, and to the left, Captain!" she called out. "That is Urbakh. There is a good broad field on the west side."

Dawson squinted ahead, and nodded absently. He knew that he was about to hit Urbakh on the nose almost any minute now, because Freddy had been doing the navigating since leaving Moscow. And when Freddy did the navigating you just naturally always hit your objective on the nose. However, he didn't mention that fact to the sharp-eyed Russian girl. He simply nodded, half smiled, and took a glance at the instrument panel.

The fact is, he was still just a little bit in what you might call a surprised trance. There just didn't seem to be anything that the Russians couldn't pull out of the hat with a snap of the fingers. Take this latest bit of Russian magic, for instance. Frankly, he had wondered about the type of plane that they were to use on the last legs of their mission. He realized that it would have to be a medium-sized bomber at least, in order to carry the number of passengers to be brought back. But he had half figured that the plane would be a Russian job. And he had hoped that he'd be able to get the feel of it in time to be able to make the tricky landing behind the Nazi Front. Also, to get it off again for the return trip.

But leave it to the Russians! They knew all the answers before you even asked the questions. And a lot of answers to a lot of questions that didn't even occur to you, too!

Five minutes after Senior Lieutenant Petrovski had returned to that front room in her mother's house, she had led Dawson and Freddy Farmer out into the night, and across a mile of wooded countryside to a billiard table smooth clearing. Presto! Russian aircraft mechanics had practically pushed up out of the ground. Presto! At an order from Senior Lieutenant Petrovski they had darted in under the branches of the bordering trees and hauled out a medium-sized bomber onto the smooth open ground. And presto! It was not a Russian plane. It was a Yank-made North American B-Twenty-Five medium bomber! A Yank lease-lend bomber that had not been converted over to Russian Air Force use.

The surprise had stunned both Dawson and Farmer speechless. In fact, like two youths living out a crazy dream, they had climbed aboard with the Senior Lieutenant to find Yank-made parachute packs, Yank-made oxygen tanks, and everything else strictly Yank from propeller hubs clear

North American B-25 Mitchell

back to the twin rudders on the tail. To slide into the pilot's seat of that B-Twenty-Five was like a ten ton weight being lifted from Dawson's shoulders. Heck! With a B-Twenty-Five he could practically land inside that cellar of Ivan Nikolsk's war-blasted farm house, if he had to. Yes, and how! Just leave it to the Russians. They knew the answers before you could even think up the questions!

"I say, want me to land it, old thing?"

Dawson snapped out of his thought trance to glance back over his shoulder at Freddy Farmer's happy grin. He shook his head violently.

"Not this time!" he snapped. "At least I want it to go into the record that we *arrived* safely at Urbakh."

"Just as you wish," the English youth chuckled. Then his face turned grave as he added, "Speaking of arriving at Urbakh safely, I wonder if we can still go on hoping for Agent Jones?"

"For me, I answer yes!" Senior Lieutenant Petrovski spoke up quickly, and touched a fingertip to a spot over her heart. "In here I think absolutely yes. No, do not laugh. When I think something inside, it is always so. This Agent Jones, he will be with us soon. He will be with us because Russia needs him to be with us. And what Russia needs, she must have. Yes! You will see."

"Okay by me!" Dawson said. "But I wasn't laughing, Senior Lieutenant. I guess that's just the way my face looks. And no cracks, Farmer! But, anyway, Senior Lieutenant, we both sure hope that you're right. This Ivan Nikolsk sure sounds like a queer guy. I've a hunch that without

Agent Jones along the three of us are going to have trouble with Ivan Nikolsk, when we find him."

"We will find him!" the Russian girl said grimly. "And if there is trouble—But what is war but bad trouble, eh?"

"Check and double check," Dawson echoed with a nod. Then, "Well, hold your hats, boys and girls. Here—Sorry, Senior Lieutenant. That's just an American expression. Anyway, here we go down for the stop-over at Urbakh."

"And I jolly well hope it will be a short one!" Freddy Farmer added, as Dawson throttled back the twin Wright "cyclones," and sent the B-Twenty-Five sliding down toward the large square-shaped field on the western edge of Urbakh.

The arrival at Urbakh of the B-Twenty-Five from Moscow was, of course, expected. And so, when Dawson landed and taxied over to the protection of some trees on the lee side of the field, a small group of Russian officers, led by an infantry Major, came out to greet them. They all seemed to know Senior Lieutenant Petrovski, and it was instantly evident that the frank admiration in their eyes and the military snappiness of their salutes was not simply because she was a pretty girl. To them she was a soldier's hero, and their every action proved it.

She introduced Dawson and Freddy to them all, but it was Major Saratov who finally accompanied them over to a house on the edge of the village. He was commander of the Russian garrison there in Urbakh, and the small house served as his headquarters. He ushered them in, and barked a request at an orderly who appeared. The orderly nodded, and beamed his pleasure, and promptly disappeared again. But only for five minutes or so. Then he returned with food and something warm to drink for them.

Up to that moment nothing but pleasantries had been spoken by anybody. But as Senior Lieutenant Petrovski picked up her warm drink, she looked across the cup at the Major.

"There is still no word from the south?" she asked quietly.

"No word at all, Senior Lieutenant," the Major said with a frown. "At Baku they are keeping constant watch, and a few planes have been sent out on the hunt, but—but so far, there has been nothing to report. It is most sad, and unfortunate."

The Russian Major bobbed his head, and stared silently at his own cup for a moment. Then he quickly raised his eyes to Nasha Petrovski's face.

"And your orders, may I ask, Senior Lieutenant?" he put the question. "You will remain here—until there is news, perhaps?"

The girl member of Soviet Intelligence gave a vigorous shake of her head.

"No, Major," she said shortly. "We have reached our own decision. Each day that passes may make it more difficult to find the person for whom we search. And too many days have gone by as it is. No. Your mechanics will look over the aircraft, and see that the tanks are full, and that everything is in readiness. And—"

The girl paused to lean over and peer up through a nearby window at the sky. A thin overcast was stealing across the surface of the cold grey-blue. She straightened up and nodded.

"Tonight there will be clouds, and no moon," she said. "It will be as good tonight for what we want as it will be any night. Yes, tonight we will cross over the enemy front to Tobolsk. And—But forgive me, Captain Dawson. You and Captain Farmer agree, yes?"

She addressed the last to Dave, who grinned and nodded.

"Absolutely, Senior Lieutenant," he said. "You're leading this parade, and what you say goes."

As the Russian girl looked just a trifle puzzled, Freddy Farmer spoke up.

"Translated into English, Senior Lieutenant," he said, "my friend means that you are in command, and that we will gladly follow your orders."

"And I'll personally see that *he* does, Senior Lieutenant!" Dawson added his bit quickly.

The Russian girl caught the byplay, and her smile flashed.

"I am honored," she said, "but this mission has three commanders, has it not? But of course. Very well, then. At midnight tonight we will take off. And now, if the Major Saratov will be so good as to produce the photographic maps that have been prepared, we will spend the rest of the time studying them, and deciding where best to land, and how to hide our aircraft from any Nazi eyes. Major?"

The Russian officer came up on his feet in nothing flat.

"At once, Senior Lieutenant," he said, and turned. "The photographic maps show every blade of grass, almost. Just to look at them is like flying over the area on a clear sunshiny day. Two seconds, Senior Lieutenant."

And it didn't take the Russian much more time than that to duck into another room, and return with a huge detail mosaic aerial map. One look at it and Dave's admiration of Russian magic went up another ten points. Major Saratov had certainly called the turn in his description of the map. It certainly was like flying over the Tobolsk area and looking down.

"So!" Senior Lieutenant Petrovski murmured as the map was placed on a table, and they all gathered around it. "If I may have your attention, Captains?"

She got it instantly, and for the next couple of hours bombs could have exploded just outside the window, and those inside would not have noticed, so engrossed were they in their study of the mosaic aerial map. Dave and Freddy had plenty of questions to ask, and they asked them. And Senior Lieutenant Petrovski had the correct answer for each question, plus a little bit of additional knowledge. In fact, by the time two hours had passed Dawson almost felt as though he'd known every little detail of the Tobolsk area all his life. It was almost as though at midnight he would make a flight back to his old home town. Russian Intelligence, plus the co-operation of Russian Aviation, had not overlooked a single thing, or passed up a single bet.

"Good grief!" Freddy Farmer gulped impulsively when they all finally straightened up from their study of the map. "There's only one blessed thing that it doesn't show. And perhaps we'll even see that if we look hard enough!"

"There is something missing, Captain?" Major Saratov asked in a hurt, disappointed tone.

"Oh, quite!" the English youth told him with a chuckle. "I fail to see Ivan Nikolsk crouching in his hiding place. But certainly everything else is clear enough."

The Russian Major let out a sound of profound relief, and laughed heartily.

"A thousand apologies for not also including that photograph, too, Captain," he said, showing his strong white teeth. "But if you so command, I will send more photograph planes over within the hour, and perhaps they will catch this Nikolsk out in an open field, eh?"

"I wouldn't bet that they wouldn't!" Dave cut in with a chuckle. "Jeepers! And to think I was a little worried about having to make a landing there in the dark. Gosh! After studying that map I could slide in there with both eyes shut."

"But please don't!" Freddy Farmer clipped at him with a broad grin. "Because I've seen some landings you've made in broad daylight with both eyes *open!*"

Dawson glanced at Major Saratov and gestured with one hand.

"Don't mind him, sir," he said in a serious tone. "He goes back into the monkey cage as soon as we return to London. Well, how about a short recess from the war, eh? And we'll get together later for a final huddle."

"Discussion of plans, he means," Freddy Farmer explained in a patient voice. "Yes, a recess might do us all good, what?"

Everybody nodded, and stood up. And then, as though invisible strings attached to each head had been pulled at the same time, each one of them turned and looked out the window facing south. And the same thought was in every mind. Agent Jones! Was he alive, or was he dead?

Several hours later all that could be seen of the sun behind the ever thickening overcast was balanced like a pale yellow ball on the western edge of the world. And even as Dawson and Farmer paused in a rambling stroll about the field, and stood still to stare at it, the bottom half of the pale yellow ball was sliced off. And then three quarters of it. And finally it wasn't there any more. There was just a faint shimmer of yellow that was quickly blotted out by the mounting overcast.

"And that's that!" Dawson grunted, more to himself than to Freddy. "If and when we see that sun again, I don't think we'll be here, anyway."

"It would be nice to think that we'll be back in Moscow, or even London, then," the English youth murmured. "But of course, that's downright silly, what? Well, I'm afraid that Senior Lieutenant Petrovski's secret inner feeling is a bit of a lost cause."

"Kind of think so myself," Dawson grunted, and turned to stare south. "Guess Agent Jones won't be with us. A tough break for him. He seemed like a swell guy at that luncheon when we met him. But anybody who went through what he did is automatically a swell guy. Did anything about him strike you, Freddy?"

"Eh? Why, certainly. That he was a very splendid sort of chap. Blast! I hate to think of him dead, and out of this. Seems so unfair, you know."

"And how!" Dawson echoed. "But that wasn't what I meant. It was about his face, his looks."

"A very good-looking face," Freddy replied. "Good grief! His good looks make you jealous, old thing? You, with the face you've got?"

"Skip it, pal!" Dawson growled. "If you missed it, then maybe I was wrong. Come on. Let's go give the crate another look-see. Boy! Am I tickled it's a Yank plane. These Russians are for my money any day in the week!"

"Wonderful people," the English youth agreed as he dropped into step. "But what did you mean by 'skip it?' What's on your mind?"

"We'll still skip it," Dawson replied stubbornly. "If it is a secret, maybe it's better to keep it that way. I don't know."

"Now, see here, my man!" Freddy Farmer snapped, and took hold of Dawson by the arm. "You—!"

But that's as far as Freddy got. At that exact moment both of them heard the roar of aircraft engines in the distance. The sound came from the south. And both, from long experience, knew instantly that British-made engines were making the noise. As one man they both froze stiff, breath locked in their lungs, and eyes frantically searched the overcast sky to the south. As usual, Freddy Farmer's eagle sharp eyes picked out the tiny moving dot sliding downward.

"There!" he cried, and flung up a pointing finger. "Just over that corner of the field. It's an R.A.F. Bristol Blenheim. Dave! Maybe it's—!"

The English youth stopped short as though not daring to speak the rest. Dawson nodded, but he too held his tongue. Together they watched the British bomber come sliding down lower and lower until it was clearly visible in every detail. And still almost not daring to breathe, they watched the twin-engined plane settle down in a beautiful landing on the field, and taxi slowly over to the North American B-Twenty-Five.

The Blenheim's wheels touching the ground seemed automatically to release hidden springs in the two boys. Together they hot-footed it over to the lee side of the field, and arrived there just as the British-marked plane was wheel braked to a stop, and the powerful twin engines cut off dead. With a wild eagerness and expectancy that made them seem like a couple of kids waiting for Santa Claus to come down the chimney, they stood there with bated breath, and saucer eyes fixed on the fuselage door. It was swung open in a moment, and a thin, good-looking fellow in oil and grease-smeared flying garb leaped lightly down on the ground and came toward them, grinning broadly.

"Greetings, you chaps!" he called out. "Been waiting for me long? I hope not."

Dawson recovered the use of his feet and his tongue first.

"Jones!" he cried, and leaped forward, hand outstretched. "Are we tickled pink to see you! Holy smokes! Look at the grey hairs we've got! We'd just about given you up for keeps. What happened? What took you so long?"

"Quite!" Freddy Farmer chipped in happily. "Dawson and I will never be the same again, I swear. Yes! What on earth happened to you?"

"Weather!" Agent Jones said with a violent nod. "Most beastly stuff that ever hit any part of the world. Right over the middle of Iran it broke. Quick! Just like that. For a spell we all thought we were goners, for sure. Jackson, he's the pilot, knew his Blenheims, though. Put us down in the middle of nowhere. And there we stayed for three days, expecting the blasted wind to turn the aircraft upside down most any minute. After the storm blew past us, it took another day to get sand and stuff out of the engine. We managed to get off early this morning. Being late, we decided not to stop at Baku. But our radio wasn't working, so we couldn't buzz Baku to tell them. We just came on, and—well, here I am."

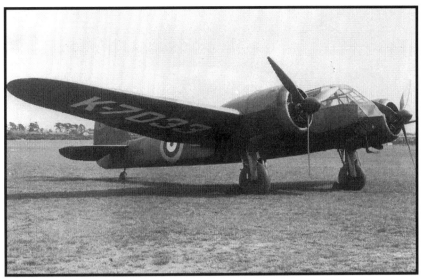

Bristol Blenheim

"And a sight for sore eyes!" Dawson cried as he stared hard at the Intelligence officer's face. "But you're in time, just in time. So come along and meet the commander of this outfit. A pretty Russian girl, believe it or not!"

"Eh, what say?" Agent Jones gasped.

"Absolutely!" Freddy Farmer spoke up. "And quite a person, too. She has killed no less than three hundred and six Nazis!"

"Good Gosh!" Jones choked out. "What a bloodthirsty damsel!"

"Not at all!" Dawson corrected him with a chuckle. "Senior Lieutenant Nasha Petrovski just doesn't like Nazis, that's all!"

CHAPTER FIFTEEN

LAND OF THE DEAD

It was just as Senior Lieutenant Petrovski had predicted. The night had no moon, and even the stars were blotted out by a five hundred foot thick layer of overcast. Pitch darkness engulfed everything in all directions. Dave Dawson couldn't see a single speck of light, save one. And that one bit of light, which was no more than a faint pale glow, was from the hooded single bulb on the instrument panel of the North American B-Twenty-Five medium bomber. Just enough light to let him read the automatic compass, and a couple of other essential instruments.

However, apart from that bit of faint light, he might well have been in the middle of a throbbing, inky dark world. The throbbing was from the two Wright Cyclone engines that were driving the B-Twenty-Five up higher and higher into the night sky. Just half an hour before he had lifted the aircraft off the square field on the western edge of Urbakh. Major Saratov, and a few other Soviet officers, had been present to wish them all well, and Godspeed back. But Dave had not missed the look half hidden in the Russian Major's eyes. And spotting that look certainly hadn't added to the joy of the dangerous flight to be undertaken. In other words, it was quite evident that Major Saratov was inwardly bidding them a very permanent farewell. Should he ever meet them again, he would undoubtedly be the most surprised man in all of the Soviet.

Whether the Russian girl officer of Soviet Intelligence, or Freddy Farmer, or Agent Jones, had noted that same look, Dawson didn't know. And, naturally, he hadn't tried to find out. If they had seen it, talking wouldn't help any. And if they hadn't, then what they didn't know wouldn't hurt them. Just the same, the little lumps of bouncing cold lead had returned to Dawson's stomach as he cleared the field and sent the B-Twenty-Five nosing upward.

Now, though, the bouncing lumps of lead were all gone. No, not because courage and all the rest of that sort of thing had driven them away. It was simply because he had other things to think about, and he was too busy to check and recheck his personal feelings. Some eighteen thousand feet of air were between the bomber's belly and the earth, and the layer of overcast now below the aircraft blotted out the ground just as completely as another layer of overcast higher up blotted out the stars.

The B-Twenty-Five was like some winged thing cutting through limitless unexplored space. In truth, those aboard had only one single contact with the world they had known. And that contact was Freddy

Farmer, who plotted every foot of the bomber's travel, and knew exactly where they were every minute of the time. In fact, it seemed to be about every other minute that the English youth leaned forward from his navigating table and handed Dave a slip of paper on which was written course corrections, or data on a new course to be flown. And at such times Dave would snap on a tiny flashlight just long enough to read the directions, and then plunge the pilot's cockpit into pitch darkness again.

Holding rigidly to the course directions that Freddy gave him, he kept his gaze fixed on the instrument panel, and tried to put everything out of his mind, save this particular job of flying. It was impossible to do that, of course. A million and one different thoughts jumped and leaped about inside his brain like so many caged up rabbits suddenly given their freedom. How soon before Freddy would give him the signal to cut the engines and start sliding down to a dead-stick landing on a piece of night-shrouded ground that he had never seen in his life before? What would be there if and when he landed the bomber? Would a chance Nazi patrol hear them, and would there be trouble? Would they be able to get away from the bomber in time? Would the tattered and torn Ukrainian peasant clothes that they all now wore be sufficient disguise? Would they be able to hide the plane? Or would they lose it, and be stranded on foot far behind the Nazi positions? Would this, and would that happen? And if so, what would be the best thing to do? And so forth, and so forth. On and on, as if beating time to the powerful throb of the Wright Cyclones.

And then, suddenly, as Dawson's brain wound up tighter and tighter like a coiled spring, he felt a hand on his shoulder, and heard Freddy Farmer's quiet voice in his ears.

"My job's finished, old thing," the English youth said. "Cut your engines, and start the glide. I've figured it as close as I possibly can, and I make it that we're ten miles from the spot. It's dead ahead, of course. But you're nose-on to a thirty mile wind. Adjust your glide angle accordingly."

"Okay, my lad!" Dawson said with far more cheerfulness than he actually felt. "Have a comfortable seat, and watch us."

"Think I'll man the tail gun, just in case," Freddy replied, with an encouraging squeeze of Dawson's shoulder. "And if it turns out to be the wrong spot, old thing, just let me know, what? I'll have another go at it."

"Sure!" Dave chuckled. "That will be swell of you, pal. If we miss and land in the middle of a Nazi camp, that landing doesn't count, huh? And why shouldn't the Nazis give us a second try? Okay, son. Trot back to your guns, but don't shoot until you see the whites of somebody's eyes, for cat's sake!"

"Quite! I understand perfectly," the English youth chuckled in reply. "And who has whites of eyes in this blasted coal mine, what? Well, luck, old thing. It's been a lovely airplane ride, you know."

With another squeeze of Dawson's shoulder, Freddy Farmer melted away in the dark, and the Yank pilot set about his delicate and dangerous task. He killed the twin Cyclones completely, and the sudden silence had the weird effect of guns going off all about him. The sensation fled him in an instant, though, and he could hear the soft whispering song of the B-Twenty-Five's wings sliding down through the darkness. Gripping the controls with hands of steel, and keeping his eyes riveted on the instrument panel, he held the bomber at the correct glide, and practically lowered it earthward a foot at a time.

Beside him, in the co-pilot's seat, was Senior Lieutenant Nasha Petrovski. Fact is, the girl had been seated there ever since the take-off. But not one word had passed her lips. It was as though she realized that this was something out of her field, and that the best way she could help was to maintain absolute silence until the aircraft was safely on the ground. And that was perfectly okay by Dawson. Not that he wouldn't have been glad to talk with the famous Russian girl. But simply because her silence helped him to forget that she was there.

Three hundred and six Nazis dead by her trigger finger, or three thousand and six. It didn't matter. She was a girl, and this was the first time Dawson had piloted a plane through war skies with other than men aboard. It was certainly a new experience, and one, he was forced to admit to himself, he would have been just as well pleased to have somebody else experience. However, she was along, of course. And so that was that.

Foot by foot Dawson took the B-Twenty-Five down toward the crest of the lower layer of overcast. Presently he thought he could make out its darker shadow just below. A glance at the altimeter told him that his eyes were not lying. In another moment he'd be going down through the stuff, and in a couple of moments after that he'd be below it and in clear night air. Then would begin the really ticklish part. Then he would see, or would not see, the dazzling white beams of Nazi searchlights groping about in the air. And then he would hear, or would not hear, the heart-chilling *crump* of exploding anti-aircraft shells. And then it would be, or would not be, the end of a very daring and crazy adventure. Then it—

With a savage shake of his head he drove the tantalizing thoughts from his brain, licked his lips and hunched forward slightly over the controls.

They were in the lower layer of overcast now. He could tell because the darkness seemed twice as profound as it had been a moment before. And then, suddenly, the B-Twenty-Five floated down out of the overcast and into clear night air. Dawson tore his gaze from the instrument panel, blinked hard as though to clear his vision, and strained his eyes ahead, and down. For a soul-torturing eternity he saw nothing but a carpet of unbroken black stretching far out in all directions. But little by little the carpet of black lost its unbroken appearance. It took on darker spots, and lighter spots, and landmarks on an aerial mosaic map re-photographed on his brain began to take shape and form.

He spotted a couple of pin points of light to the left, and a long curving dark shadow. The curving shadow he knew was a stretch of woods on the east side of Urbakh. And the pin points of light he was certain came from the village itself. Then, as he saw a winding lighter shadow, his heart swelled with pride. Trust old Freddy Farmer! Old Freddy could guide you halfway around the world to a dime you had left in the middle of a desert. That winding lighter shadow was a tributary of the Don River. And when his eyes picked out the eastern and lower part of an S that the tributary formed, he would then be looking at the small, wood-bordered patch of flat ground where he would dead-stick land the bomber. Or at least he would be looking at a spot of wood-bordered flat ground that *Had* been that when the Russian aerial photographs were taken.

So tensed and keyed up was Dawson that when Senior Lieutenant Petrovski suddenly reached out and gripped his arm he almost let out a startled yell. He curbed it in time, however, so his own voice didn't drown out the words the Russian girl spoke.

"There, a little to the left!" she called out. "You see it, Captain Dawson? Where the little river makes that turn to the right? That is the place."

It took Dawson all of five seconds to pick out the spot, and when he did he silently saluted the Russian girl at his side.

"Yes, I see it, Senior Lieutenant," he told her. Then to himself, "You and Freddy Farmer! Eagle eyes!"

Perhaps it was a good thing that the Russian girl had spoken. At any rate, the tenseness and the tightness went out of Dawson. A cool calm settled over him, and it was though he were simply making an emergency night landing in some familiar place. But, of course, a night landing without the benefit of landing lights!

Actually, though, it was going to be considerably more than just putting the B-Twenty-Five down on the ground. When his wheels finally touched, he must have enough forward speed to carry him as close to the bordering trees as possible. There would be no "dolly-tractor" to haul the bomber over the ground. And those aboard certainly didn't possess the strength to move the bomber around as you'd hoist up the tail of a pursuit ship and move it. And, of course, to start up the engines and taxi close to the bordering trees was definitely out of the question. Might just as well send the Nazis in the neighborhood a telegram that they were coming, and at what time. And so—

The rambling thoughts in Dawson's brain slid off into oblivion. The darker shadow of the ground was directly beneath his cranked down wheels now. And dead ahead was the darker shadow, too, of the bordering trees at the far end of the field. It was now or never. Success, or a beautiful crack-up that would bring Nazis on the jump from miles around. Dawson swallowed impulsively, and in the last few split seconds of time allowed, every event, big and small, of his entire existence on earth seemed to flash across the screen of his brain.

And then the wheels touched. The B-Twenty-Five tried to bounce back up a little into the air, but an expert had set it on the ground, and the twin tail came down to touch and cling to the earth also. Sweat was pouring off Dawson's face, but he didn't bother wiping it off so that it wouldn't run into his eyes. Like a statue of solid stone, he sat hunched in the seat, letting the bomber trundle forward, and keeping his gaze fixed on the dark shadow of trees ahead.

It seemed as though a thousand years dragged by while that B-Twenty-Five rolled forward over the ground. But finally the bordering trees loomed up large and ominous just ahead of the nose. Dawson applied the wheel brakes, and the forward movement of the bomber slackened off considerably. And at the very last moment he took off the right wheel brake, but held the left steady so that the bomber pivoted around to that side, and finally stopped in a position where another half-turn was all that was needed for them to be able to use the entire length of the field for a take-off.

"Well, Jap-knife me in the back if we didn't make it!" Dave gasped joyfully as the bomber's wheels made their last half-turn. "Here we are, anyway."

"And accomplished by the ace of aces, Captain Dawson!" the Russian girl spoke up. "But there is no time for compliments now. There is work for all of us. We must hurry, so that when dawn comes there will be no sign to be seen from the air."

"Huh?" Dawson grunted. "What was that, Senior Lieutenant?"

"This aircraft!" she said with a startling sharpness in her voice. "We must cover it with branches and bushes, so that Nazi airmen will not see that it is here. Is that not so?"

"That is absolutely correct!" Dawson replied instantly, and heaved up out of his seat. "And I am very glad that there is at least *one* brain in this outfit. My apologies for my dumbness, Senior Lieutenant. Let's go!"

CHAPTER SIXTEEN
SATAN IS GLEEFUL

The new dawn was a pale band of light that etched the eastern rim of the world. The overcast layers that had filled the night sky were fast breaking up and dissolving into nothingness. It was a sure sign that the new day would be clear and bright. And as Dave Dawson stared up at the slowly changing sky, he tried to tell himself that that was a very good sign, and that everything would turn out swell.

Yes, he was trying to tell himself and convince himself, but he didn't even come close. The hand of invisible doom and disaster seemed to be pressing down hard on his heart. And countless demons of doubt and dread and misgiving were dancing around in his brain. He shifted his position on the floor and stared over at Freddy Farmer and Agent Jones, who sat back-propped and silent against the room wall.

Room wall? Well, it could hardly be called that. The place where the three of them were now was little more than a hundred year old cow-shed sunk half into the ground from changing weather, and just plain natural deterioration. It was a good half-mile from the spot where they had left the B-Twenty-Five bomber well camouflaged, covered by tree branches, bushes, and anything else that they could lay their hands on. To this tumbled down mess of rotted wood Senior Lieutenant Petrovski had led them as straight as though she were walking a piece of taut string. Then, she had *left* them here well over two hours ago!

Yes! Left them to cool their heels, and bite their fingernails if they wished, while she went out into the darkness to scout about the village of Urbakh, and find out just what the picture was. When she had told them of her intention, a whole batch of arguments had leaped to Dawson's lips, just as they had leaped to the lips of Freddy Farmer, and Agent Jones. However, the Russian girl was quick to read what was in their minds. And she asked them a question that put an end to all the arguments, and stopped them all cold.

"And who but I, who knows this area as a birthplace, should go out and find what should be done next?" she had asked.

And *was* there one of them better qualified to look over the lay of the land? There was not! However, Dawson had been tempted to insist that he go along with her, just as a matter of protection, so to speak. But before he spoke he thought of three hundred and six Nazis who wouldn't help Hitler any more. So he didn't even speak.

However, the girl officer of Russian Intelligence had said that she would return in a little over an hour. And it was now well over *two* hours since she had slipped away in the darkness like a greased shadow. That wasn't so good, and the demons of doubt and dread and misgiving were loudly clamoring for recognition in Dawson's brain.

"I fancy we're all thinking the same thoughts, what?" Freddy Farmer's low voice suddenly broke the silence. "And deucedly unpleasant thoughts, too."

"Check!" Dawson muttered grimly. "I'm afraid we were dopes to let her go out alone, even if she does know this neck of the woods, and how to take care of any Nazis she bumps into."

"Oh, she'll be back," Agent Jones spoke up confidently. "The Russian women are every bit as good at waging war as the Russian men, you know."

"Sure!" Dawson grunted. "But a lot of Russian men soldiers have been shot in this war. However—well, I guess the only thing we can do is wait some more."

"And if she doesn't show up at all?" Freddy Farmer put the obvious question. "Then what?"

"Then I haven't the faintest idea," Dawson replied with a heavy sigh. "We'll just have to think up something if and when that time arrives."

"We could go to the Nazi Commandant hereabouts, and ask him if he knows where we could find Nikolsk," Agent Jones offered with a chuckle.

"Thanks for the attempt at humor!" Dawson groaned. "But I don't feel like laughing. I feel like—Hold it! You hear that, fellows?"

There was no need to ask the question. Even a deaf man could have heard the thunderous roar of revving aircraft engines that suddenly blasted the silence of dawn to the four winds. As though controlled by invisible strings, the three of them leaped to their feet and crowded over to the glassless window on the side of the room nearest the location of the sound. It did them little good, however. They simply found themselves staring out at a wall of trees that blocked off even the growing light of dawn.

That didn't matter very much, though. And it certainly didn't cause their hearts to thump less violently. The three of them knew at once that the roaring was from German aircraft engines. And the three of them also realized at once that a Nazi flying field couldn't be more than a few hundred yards away!

"Sweet tripe!" Dawson gasped when he could catch his breath. "Did we pick a nice secluded out of the way spot, I don't think! That's a Nazi flying field. And those engines sound like Messerschmitt One-Nines and One-Tens to me!"

"Quite!" Agent Jones grunted, tight-lipped. "Certainly isn't a tank base. A Jerry airdrome, without a doubt. And here come some of the blighters off on the early patrol!"

The last statement was quite true. Hardly had the words left Agent Jones' lips when six Messerschmitt One-Tens went tearing by no more than three hundred feet over the spot where the three youths crouched hidden. A moment later a second flight of Nazi planes roared by toward the front. And then a third flight, and a fourth. Dawson squinted up at each flight, and saw that his guess had been correct. Half of the planes were single-seater Messerschmitt One-Nine fighters. And the other half were Messerschmitt One-Tens. And when the last flight had passed over he sat down on the floor again, scowled darkly, and scratched his head.

"Just ducky, just dandy!" he groaned. "We hide our ship just a hop skip and a jump from a mess of high speed Nazi jobs. What a sweet hope we'd have trying to take off. Or is there some way of getting a B-Twenty-Five into the air without using the engines?"

"Lots of ways!" Freddy Farmer grunted unhappily. "But I can't seem to think of one, right now."

"Well, keep thinking, pal!" Dawson told him. "Because I guess we're going to have to do just that. Darn it! Where is that Senior Lieutenant, anyway? She's one bright girl, and always has the right answer. Maybe she'll have the right answer to this one."

"I hope!" Agent Jones echoed fervently.

"I fancy that makes two of us who hope, old thing," Freddy Farmer sighed. "A bit strange, though, there was no sign of the airfield on that mosaic map of Major Saratov's," he went on after a split second pause. "Or could all of us have been so blind as to have missed it?"

"Hardly," Agent Jones said with a grim laugh. "If you ask me, we didn't spot it because you wouldn't even spot it from the air. The Jerries, as you well know, are absolutely top-hole in the art of camouflaging. I think that's the answer, frankly. A very cleverly camouflaged air base that Soviet pilots haven't discovered yet."

"And we have—too late!" Dawson grunted. "Say, listen, you two. What say we give the Senior Lieutenant twenty minutes more, and if she hasn't returned by then we go take a look-see at that airfield, huh? To my way of thinking, we can't count too much on the B-Twenty-Five, with a nest of Messerschmitts this close. Better have a look-see, anyway. Am I right, or wrong?"

"Perfectly right!" Freddy Farmer said.

"The same for me," Agent Jones echoed. "Twenty minutes more for the lady to show up, and then we start snooping around on our own."

Whether the war gods planned it that way or not will of course never be known. But exactly nineteen minutes had ticked by on Dave Dawson's wrist watch when suddenly a shadow fell across the dawn light on the floor, and Senior Lieutenant Nasha Petrovski came gliding into the room. Instantly the three men were on their feet, and it was Dawson who found his tongue first.

"Boy! Am I glad to see you, lady!" he gulped out impulsively. "I mean, Senior Lieutenant, it's sure nice to see you back. We were getting mighty worried."

The Russian girl smiled her thanks, but her smile was far from her usual flashing one. She sat down on the floor and pulled off her tattered peasant cap to show her close cropped jet black hair. Dawson, staring at her for a moment, could not help but admit to himself that Nasha Petrovski in a Senior Lieutenant's snappy uniform, or Nasha Petrovski in the tattered garments of a Ukrainian peasant woman, was still one mighty pretty girl. He brushed the flash thought from his brain, however, and squatted down on his heels in front of her.

"Bad news, eh, Senior Lieutenant?" he asked quietly. "I think I can see it in your face."

She didn't answer him for a moment. She seemed content to wait until Freddy Farmer and Agent Jones had also squatted down on the floor. Then she nodded her head, and her eyes flashed with some inner rage.

"Yes, bad news, my gallant comrades," she said evenly. "It would seem the Nazis here at Urbakh are far more clever than we expected."

"Quite," Agent Jones murmured politely. "The camouflaged airfield. We have just been watching some of their planes fly over."

"Yes, a secret airfield!" the Russian girl said in a low voice, and clenched her two hands into fists. "It is not a quarter of a mile from where we now sit. I have seen it, and though I will hate all Nazis to my death, I must speak praise of that secret field. It is all underground, under a large flat-topped hill. You almost stumble into it before you see the screens of branches that hang down over the entrance. When planes are to take off, the screens are lifted by wire cables and the valley at the base of the hill becomes a smooth take-off runway. It is clever. Yes, it is ingenious. It is also most unlucky for us that Nazis are so close."

"Well, they haven't spotted us yet!" Dawson said, to cheer her up a little. "And we'll just make sure that they don't."

"Yes, of course," the Russian girl replied in a dull voice, and shrugged sort of hopelessly. "But it is blame that I must put on my own shoulders. I am ashamed to—"

"Now look, Senior Lieutenant!" Dave spoke up quickly. "We—"

But that's as far as he could get. She silenced him with her eyes, and an upraised hand.

"Let me finish, please, Captain Dawson," she said. "Then you will realize why I am so ashamed. It is my sad duty to report to you three gallant ones that the Nazis have *already* discovered our airplane. There is a strong guard about it this very minute. And, of course, they realize that we must be somewhere in this area."

Had Hitler himself stepped through the cockeyed slanting doorway at that exact moment, the three youths wouldn't have been much more stunned. To Dawson it was like something exploding inside his head. And quick as a flash he thought of the incident aboard the Flying Scotsman, and of the air battle just before the Wellington's arrival in Moscow. Was it true? Was it true that the Gestapo had been here all the time waiting for them? Had they seen or heard the B-Twenty-Five sliding down for the night landing, and just waited for daylight to capture it? Was that the truth? Dawson wondered. He wondered hard, and little by little he began to get the feeling that the Nazis didn't know who, or how many, had arrived in their midst. If so, why had they not swooped down on the landed plane instantly, and shot or captured everybody right then and there? Was it because they had not been able to reach the bomber before its crew had slipped away in the darkness? Or was it because they, themselves, hoped to be led to the hiding place of one Ivan Nikolsk, who was such an important link in the revealing of their war plans?

Dawson wondered and pondered in silence, and then suddenly he was conscious of Freddy Farmer speaking.

"Let them have the blasted aircraft, and welcome to it!" the English-born air ace was saying. "It makes matters a bit more difficult, but far from impossible. I fancy that there isn't one of us who hasn't been stranded behind Nazi lines before this. We'll get away from the beggars, somehow. The main thing is to locate this bloke, Ivan Nikolsk, and let Agent Jones, here, do his share in this balmy show we're to pull off."

"But that will not be so easy, either, I am most sad to report," Senior Lieutenant Petrovski said bitterly. "A little luck has been mine since I last saw you. I found Ivan Nikolsk, and it was easier than I had dared hope. There was a certain house I went to, on the east side of the village. An old woman, too old to interest the Nazis. Nina, her name is. She used to rock me in my cradle. She made for me my first doll, out of thin air and a bit of string, almost. She was there at the house. Half blind, but she knew me at once. She swore that she knew in her heart that I was coming. Perhaps yes. Who is there to say no? And what is planned for us on this earth, and what is not planned for us? Who is there to prove this or that to be wrong, or a miracle?"

The Russian girl suddenly caught herself up and made a little apologetic gesture with her hands.

"But such mysteries of life are not for us to speak of at the moment," she continued. "It is just that Ivan Nikolsk went to Nina for hiding. He is there. He is there now. I saw him."

"Oh, splendid!" Freddy Farmer burst out excitedly. "Did you speak to him, Senior Lieutenant? And what did he say to you? By Jove!"

"No." She turned to the English youth with a sad smile. "I have made you happy only to make you unhappy. I spoke to Ivan Nikolsk, but he did not speak to me. He is unconscious. He has been so for four days. He has illness, and a terrible fever. Nina has done what she could. But there is no doctor, and it would mean her life to go to the Nazis in the village. Nina says that he has not long to live. And I have seen him, and so believe her!"

CHAPTER SEVENTEEN
END OF THE BEGINNING

The echo of Senior Lieutenant Petrovski's words seemed to linger tauntingly for ages and ages. Nobody else spoke. Nobody could think of anything to say. The stillness of dawn stole in through the broken and shattered windows, and lent to the place the atmosphere of a long abandoned tomb. Dawson tried desperately to think of something to say—anything that would remove a little of the bitterness that was stamped all over the Russian girl's face. Not one bit of what had happened was her fault, but that didn't make any difference to her. She accepted the fault as her own, and it showed plainly in the bitter look on her face.

"Well, that just tightens things up a little," the words finally came to his tongue, and popped off. "We've just got to shift into high gear a little sooner. The big idea now is to get Ivan Nikolsk to a good Russian hospital, and get him there fast. Right?"

"True enough," Freddy Farmer grunted, and stared at him hard. "But I fancy there are one or two little details to be worked out, what?"

"Right!" Dawson shot right back at him. "And that's where you and I can earn a little of what they pay us. Look, Senior Lieutenant, just where is this Nina's house? Can you tell me exactly, so I'd recognize it when I saw it?"

"But of course!" the Russian girl replied, and brightened up a little. "It was in that mosaic aerial map. You recall those two roads that formed a Y by those star-shaped fields? You remember speaking about the shape of those fields, eh? It is that house right there in the top part of that Y."

"Check!" Dawson cried eagerly, as he instantly pin pointed the spot on the memory picture of that aerial map in his brain. "Yes! I know just where it is. Now, another question. Are there many Nazis roaming around here? I mean, could you and Agent Jones get to this Nina's house without being stopped and picked up?"

"The Nazis would never see us!" the Russian girl said almost scornfully. "Too many times have I—"

"Okay, and sorry," Dawson stopped her with a grin. "I didn't mean that the way you took it. Okay, then. Answer me this, if you will? Could Farmer and I get to that house without being nailed?"

The Russian girl flashed him a searching look, and then laughed softly.

"What a Russian girl can do, the Captains Dawson and Farmer can certainly do!" she said. "And much more skilfully, no doubt."

Dawson hesitated the fraction of a second, half expecting a crack from Freddy. But the situation was too serious for the English youth to loosen his tongue in a retort.

"Well, that's all I want to know," Dawson finally said with a grin. "Now look, Senior Lieutenant. You and Agent Jones slide over to this Nina's house, and get ready to move Nikolsk out of there. You know, wrap him up in blankets, if there're any around. But, more important, try to check on the movements of any Nazis who might be around. Meanwhile Farmer and I—well, we're going to take a little walk. However, we'll join you and Agent Jones as soon as we can. But it might not be until nightfall tonight. So don't get worried if we take that long."

"I say, what's up old thing?" Agent Jones broke into the conversation. "Just what do you and Farmer plan to do? A walk to where, may I ask?"

"Sure, go ahead and ask it," the Yank air ace chuckled. "The answer is that I am not quite sure, right now. However, the B-Twenty-Five is out for us, now. So Farmer's and my job will be to dig up some other means of travel, and dig it up in a hurry. We'll do our darnedest, anyway. And I promise, we'll both show up at Nina's sooner or later. So is it okay for us to split forces and get to work? Or has one of you something better thought up?"

None of the other three seemed to think much of Dawson's suggestion for action. The looks on their faces showed it. But not one of them could think of any better suggestion, so no protests or arguments were forthcoming. Dawson gave them three long minutes to think of something. Then he nodded, and stood up.

"Okay, time flies!" he said. "The Senior Lieutenant, and Agent Jones, head for Nina's house, and get Nikolsk ready for travel. And maybe you'll get a break, Jones. Maybe Nikolsk will come to long enough to recognize you and do some talking. That's why I think you should go with the Senior Lieutenant instead of with us, see?"

"But of course!" Jones gasped as his face reddened slightly. "I didn't think. Naturally. Sorry, Dawson."

"Skip it, pal," the Yank grinned at him. Then, stabbing a finger at Freddy Farmer, he said, "Boy! On your feet, and come with Papa. And watch those big feet, too. The less noise, the better our chances."

"Really?" the English youth snorted, and made a face. "Well, if it wasn't for the situation, and the fact a young lady is present, I'd tell you, my good man, to—"

"But of course you won't!" Dawson shot at him. "So pipe down, sweetheart, and let's get going. By nightfall at the latest, you two. Keep your fingers crossed!"

With a grin and a wave of his hand at Senior Lieutenant Petrovski and Agent Jones, Dawson turned and led the way out through the slanting doorway, and sharp left into the thick woods that edged that side of the house. He kept going until he was a good two hundred yards deep in the woods. Then he slid to the ground and crawled into some of the heavy undergrowth. Freddy Farmer crawled in right beside him, and even in the bad light Dawson could see the library full of questions that gleamed in his pal's eyes.

"Easy does it, sweetheart," Dave said softly, and held up a restraining hand. "I know you think I'm nuts, pal. But I couldn't very well explain everything in there. Besides, I wouldn't be able to explain everything, because I haven't caught all the angles yet myself."

"Yes, you are quite balmy, or seem so," the English youth replied with a gesture. "But I've seen you just as balmy in one or two other tight corners. So I'll wait and listen before I make up my mind one way or the other. Well, just what is steaming in that head of yours?"

"The word is cooking, not steaming," Dawson chuckled. "But skip it. Look, Freddy. As I get the picture, the Nazis—Gestapo, or maybe no Gestapo—have stolen the play from us. Naturally, if they've found the B-Twenty-Five, as the Senior Lieutenant says, they know for sure that there is somebody behind their lines. Right? Okay. However, I've got a feeling that there is one thing they *don't* know."

"Go on," Freddy Farmer grunted as Dawson paused. "What?"

"They don't know *how many* of us are here," the Yank replied quickly.

"But the B-Twenty-Five must indicate to them that—!" the English youth managed to say before Dawson interrupted.

"Sure, but so what? That bomber can mean one of two things to them. That it brought over a full crew to do something. Or that a couple of guys flew it over to take *others* back. And if the Gestapo is mixed up in this, they must feel sure that the B-Twenty-Five is here to take others back."

"Which is just about the truth," the English youth grunted gloomily.

"So that's just why we've got to step in and make them change their minds!" Dawson shot at him. "We've got to make them think that only two of us came over, and, finding out that our plans were shot high wide and handsome because the bomber was captured, that we called off the deal and lit out for home as fast as we could. See?"

"I most certainly don't see!" Freddy Farmer growled, and scowled. "What kind of raving is this, anyway?"

"Too bad I haven't got a pencil!" Dawson grated. "I could draw you a picture. Stop thinking of food, and concentrate, will you, pal?"

"I'll take you up on that remark later!" Freddy snapped. "Of course I'm concentrating. But are you talking sense?"

"I'll try to put it in words of no more than five letters," Dave sighed. "Now, here it is. We must make them think that only two people came over in that B-Twenty-Five. Two guys, who planned to make a secret landing at night and pick up—well, pick up one, or two, or half a dozen other people on this side. The Nazis can pick their own number from one to ten. Okay. The bomber is captured by them, so we've got to make them think we got scared, called off what we had hoped to accomplish, and beat it back to the safety of the Russian front. Got it, so far?"

"Yes, I think so," Freddy replied. "So far. But how do you propose to make them think we've given up and gone back? And just how do you plan for us to go back?"

Dawson jerked a thumb off to the right.

"That very trick airdrome of theirs," he said shortly. "And a couple of those single-seater Messerschmitt One-Nines. We—"

"But a Messerschmitt One-Ten will carry two!" the English youth interrupted. "In fact, they carry a radioman, also, which makes three."

"My, how you know your airplanes!" Dawson snapped. "Shut up, and listen, will you? Two single-seaters will mean to them that only *two* guys are on their way home. So they'll naturally figure that *only two guys* came over in the B-Twenty-Five, see? So, as I was saying, we swipe two single-seaters from their trick airdrome and high-tail for the Russian front. And—Now, keep your shirt on, and let me finish! And of course they come chasing after us. Well, we let them get a good look at us taking it on the lam. Get—"

"*Lam*, Dave? I—"

"So your education's been neglected, but skip it for now!" the Yank said quickly. "We let them see us escape. Let them see us get well over Russian-held ground, so they are forced to turn back. Well, a few minutes later we do the same thing, see? We've got to work it so it'll be almost dark by then. Anyway, we breeze back, kill our engines, and make a dead-stick landing in *that field close to Nina's house.* The Nazis, thinking that we've given them the slip, will probably relax the guard on the B-Twenty-Five. So at Nina's house we pick up the others, sneak back, and rush the one or two guards that have been left with the bomber. We take care of them, pile aboard, and off we go to a Moscow hospital with Nikolsk. And who knows? Maybe by then Agent Jones will have learned everything from the poor devil's own lips. Well? Okay, or does it smell? And if so, then you tell one, pal!"

"It's all quite mad, of course," the English youth said after a long moment of silence. "However, it's no more barmy, I fancy, than a few other things we've tried, and we've always managed to come out on top so far. There are three big question marks, though. One, can we steal the two single-seaters? Two, can we land near Nina's house without being seen, or heard? And three, will they reduce the guard over the bomber so that we can overpower them quickly enough? After all, we only have an automatic apiece. However—"

Freddy paused and shrugged. And Dawson nodded, and grinned.

"Check!" he said. "There's only one way we can find out those answers. That's to take a crack at it."

"And I always did like London at this time of the year," Freddy Farmer murmured softly with a long sigh.

CHAPTER EIGHTEEN
ACES DON'T WAIT

A s though the gods of good fortune, and Lady Luck, were well informed of what was to take place in the Tobolsk area, and wished to add their bit of help, dull grey clouds began to form in the western sky shortly after noon. And by three o'clock the sun was hidden completely, and shadowy, misty light filled the heavens, and covered the earth like a thin shroud.

Hugging the ground under a mass of leafy bushes, Dave Dawson and Freddy Farmer breathed silent prayers of thanks for the helpful change in the weather, and in between prayers asked only that four Nazi airplane mechanics might complete their routine chores, and go elsewhere out of sight. The four Nazi mechanics were no more than sixty yards from where the two boys hugged the damp ground, and they were giving their attention to three Messerschmitt One-Nines, and half a dozen Messerschmitt One-Tens lined up under a wide spread of overhanging tree branches that hid them completely from the air. Just beyond the planes, and to the right, rose a squat, flat-topped hill. Even from where the boys hugged the ground the hill looked just like that—squat, and flat-topped. But they knew different. Not only because of what they had guessed, and heard from Senior Lieutenant Petrovski's lips, but also from what they had seen with their own eyes!

Just one hour previously they had reached this spot and crouched down to study the scene, and wait for their big opportunity—if and when it came. Up until an hour ago they had covered a considerable area of Nazi-occupied Russian ground. A portion of it, because of the necessity of changing course to avoid personal contact with Nazi patrols, or groups of Luftwaffe pilots out stretching their legs after a flight over the front, and for a few other less important reasons. But a certain portion of it they had covered on purpose, mainly to have a look at the guarded B-Twenty-Five bomber. But that look had not added to their peace of mind, or to their hopes.

They had learned that not only was a heavy guard posted close to the bomber—which, incidentally, was inspected practically every five minutes by a new group of Luftwaffe pilots—but a ring of guards had also been thrown out about the bomber at a considerable distance. In other words, the Nazis were taking no chances on a surprise rushing attack. Those whom they were obviously expecting would be forced to break through two rings of defense to reach the aircraft. No, a good look from a safe distance at the B-Twenty-Five had not given them cause to so much as murmur with happiness. If that guard was *not* reduced, and by two thirds at the most, they were slated to have one terrific job on their hands. One terrific job, and a very hopeless one, too.

However, time alone would reveal what was to be, and what wasn't to be. So they had left the picture just as it was, and gone on about their "travels." And now they hugged the ground, and kept their eyes fixed on four Nazi mechanics, and by the very intensity of their stares tried to make the four square-heads stop fiddling around with the Messerschmitts and go away.

"Almost as though they knew we were here," Freddy Farmer muttered under his breath, "and were purposely taking as long as they could. Blast them, anyway!"

"I can think of a lot of other things to call those tramps!" Dawson grated softly. "And if you want the truth, I'm having a tough time fighting down the yen to tear into them, anyway. They don't look like they're armed."

"But no doubt each one of the blighters has a Luger in his coverall pocket," Freddy Farmer murmured. "I fancy the Nazis have learned not to go around unarmed *any* place in Russia. Quite!"

Dawson started to nod and echo that very truthful surmise, but at that moment he heard one of the mechanics shout something, and his heart started pounding furiously against his ribs. He didn't catch the words, but he didn't have to. Actions told him all he needed to know. The actions of the four mechanics who promptly quit work, and went walking over toward the base of the squat, flat-topped hill. A moment or two later Dawson and Freddy Farmer witnessed for the second time in an hour a bit of Nazi-made ingenuity. For the second time in an hour, they witnessed what Senior Lieutenant Nasha Petrovski had told them about.

In short, they watched the four mechanics walk to the base of the hill, watched a section of "hill" swing outward and upward a little way, and the four mechanics walk into the hill, and then saw the camouflage screening drop back into place again. A sudden and quite insane desire to have a look at all that was inside that hill surged through Dawson. But, naturally, he killed the urge even as it was born, and simply promised himself that if he lived through the war, he would come back for a real inspection of this spot after it was all over.

"Well, don't look right now," he breathed softly, and pushed up onto his hands and knees, "but I think it's time for us to part company for a spell. Freddy, old pal, you hop for that first crate, and I'll hop for the one right next to it. Meet you in the air, kid. And don't wait to ask permission to take off, see? You won't get it!"

"Not likely!" the English-born air ace grinned back at him, tight-lipped. "And keep your mind on your own knitting, old thing. A One-Nine is a bit of all right, but a tricky beggar, you know."

"Yeah, I once read that in a book!" Dave growled. Then, throwing Farmer a wink, "This is it, pal. And don't spare the horses!"

And that was that. No handclasp, and no last words of planning. There was no need for either. Each knew exactly how the other felt. And each knew exactly what the other planned to do, and would do—unless Death stopped him.

And so, like a couple of bolts of lightning ripping out from the center of a thunderhead, the two boys ripped up out from under the sheltering bushes, and went streaking straight across sixty yards of open ground. To anybody watching them it must have seemed that their feet didn't even touch the ground; that they were just a couple of cannon shells en route. And as Dave reached the side of the cockpit of his Messerschmitt One-Nine, it became instantly evident that somebody had been watching them, or at least had suddenly spotted Freddy and himself, because there was the sound of a muffled shout of wild alarm, followed almost instantly by the heart-chilling chatter of a machine gun. However, Dave didn't hear the whine of bullets, and he didn't bother to wait to see if a second burst would come closer. His feet just up and left the ground, and he practically shot down through the cockpit hatch opening to the seat.

Even as he landed, hard, his hands were in furious motion. In what was little more than the continuation of a single movement he whipped up the ignition switch, snapped on the booster magneto, and punched the starter button as he rammed the throttle open. One—two—three horrible seconds dragged by, and then the Daimler-Benz engine in the nose caught in a mighty thunder of sound. And as it did so he kicked off the wheel brakes and opened the throttle wide, breathing a prayer of gratitude to the four mechanics for having tested the engine and thus warmed it up for him.

Like a race horse leaving the barrier, Dawson's Messerschmitt went streaking out from under the cover of overhanging branches and down the flat strip of valley. Out the corner of his eye he caught a glimpse of Freddy Farmer also in motion in the other plane. A song of joy burst out in his heart, and he impulsively lifted a hand in a derisive gesture at the machine guns yammering savagely behind him.

"Didn't realize you were guarding the wrong aircraft, did you, tramps?" he shouted aloud, and pulled the Messerschmitt clear of the ground. "Well, now, isn't that just too bad! But we'll wait for you, if you want, hey, Freddy, old kid?"

Of course, the English youth couldn't hear the words, but it wasn't necessary. As planned, both youths throttled slightly, once they got the planes up out of range of the machine gun fire. They did so to give the Nazis plenty of time to race out of the hill hangar and over to the line of planes. Looking back, Dawson saw them, and a happy grin stretched his lips. So far, so good! Now to keep just enough ahead of those bums, and then lose them when well over the Russian front.

"And then Freddy and I will really go to work!" Dawson grunted grimly, and veered around toward the north. "Wonder what tomorrow will be like? Yeah! And *if* I'll see it!"

With a shrug, and a shake of his head, he knocked the thought into oblivion, and, after glancing over at Freddy on his right, fixed his gaze on the northern horizon.

A little under an hour later a conglomeration of emotions was surging through Dawson. Russian-held ground was under his wings now. Russian ground, and he had only to throttle his Daimler-Benz and slide down to complete safety. But, of course, that thought didn't even cut a tiny corner in his brain. It wasn't even born, for the very simple reason that the job wasn't even half finished. True, they were over Russian ground, and a couple of minutes before the pursuing Nazis had given up the chase as a lost cause and swung all the way around to the south, to be speedily lost to view in the ever approaching shadows of nightfall. Yes, all that was water under the bridge so far. But half the job, and the most dangerous half was still waiting to be accomplished.

"So get on with it, as Freddy would say," Dawson grunted, and waggled his wings just before he banked around toward the south.

The English youth swung around right after him, and in wing-tip formation they headed toward the southeast. For some five long minutes they droned along. And then, just as they were passing over the last of the Russian advance positions on that section of the front, Dawson sat up stiff and straight in the seat. His eyes had spotted a moving dot silhouetted against the bleak, cheerless sky of coming night. It grew bigger and bigger, and finally took on the shape and outline of a Messerschmitt!

Dawson squinted at it for a second or so longer, and then when the Nazi craft suddenly veered off to the west, and headed up toward the clouds, he took a quick look over at Freddy, and started to bark out a signal burst from his guns.

There was no need for that, however. The English youth had already spotted the plane, and was hauling his ship around and up after it. Dawson grinned, and yanked his own One-Nine around and up in Freddy's wake.

"Leave it to you, Eagle Eyes!" he shouted. "Okay, pal. He sure is our baby. Hanging around so he can learn things, maybe, and then go tearing back to tell them all about it. Well, not today, eh, Freddy?"

With a grim nod for emphasis, Dawson jammed the heel of his palm against the already wide open throttle, and kept his gaze fixed on the third Nazi plane streaking upward for the clouds. For what seemed like all eternity the lumps of cold lead bounced around in Dawson's stomach. If they lost that Nazi there was no telling what might happen. Maybe he was just some pilot up on a test flight, but his sudden dash for the seclusion of the clouds didn't bear that out. No. More likely he had been left aloft to keep watch, and to see if those who had escaped made any attempt to return. Sure, and maybe that was a very cockeyed view for Dawson to take, too. However, there was no way of telling one way or the other. So that left only one thing to do. To knock off that Nazi just in case he was aloft for no good purpose.

"But in this bum light?" Dawson grated. "Not so good! If he reaches those clouds, we'll never find him. Five minutes more, and night will be here in earnest. And we'll—"

He never finished the rest. He didn't because at that moment it was his privilege to witness something that few war pilots ever see in their lifetime—in short, a perfect long range shot smacking home. Once in maybe a billion times a burst of aerial machine gun bullets hit their mark at the extreme end of their range. All the other times they fly wide, or spend themselves downward toward earth.

But this was one of those once in a billion times, and the burst of bullets came from the guns on Freddy Farmer's Messerschmitt. Dawson hadn't even rested his thumb on his trigger trip because of the seemingly hopeless distance to the target. However, Freddy Farmer had taken a bead, and his bit of perfect aerial shooting proved to be in a class all by itself. The "target" lurched off to the left, as though it had been sliding along an invisible greased pole, and had slid off. It dropped right down to the vertical, and then suddenly smoke and livid red flame belched out and up from its nose. Hardly daring to believe his eyes, Dawson watched the bit of blazing doom clear down to where it disappeared from view behind a ridge. And a split second later, a fountain of flashing orange and red told him that the plane had struck earth.

"Nope, it didn't happen!" he told himself in a dazed voice. "Things like that just don't happen. You only read about them in stories. Sweet tripe! How I love that guy, Freddy Farmer. Compared to him, am I a bum!"

With a vigorous nod for emphasis, he veered over closer to the English youth's plane and lifted his clasped hands high above his head in the gesture of a boxer saluting the crowd.

"You for me, sweetheart!" he shouted into the roar of his engine. "Now, let's go and pull off the last of the miracles!"

The words had no more than left his lips, however, when he happened to stare toward the east—and swallowed hard. Pitch black storm clouds were hurtling up out of the east, and swiftly blotting out the last fading tints of day much as a descending blanket blots out the flickering flame of a candle. In a matter of minutes, now, Freddy and he wouldn't be able to spot Nina's house in the darkness, much less make safe landings close by!

CHAPTER NINETEEN
HEADACHES FOR HITLER

Dawson glanced impulsively over at Freddy Farmer, and quickly realized that the English youth had spotted the approaching storm clouds, too, and obviously had the same thoughts. Because even as their eyes met Freddy nodded violently, and banked around, and stuck his nose down in the general direction of the eastern side of the village of Tobolsk, just out of sight over the horizon.

"Well, there's one thing, anyway," Dawson grunted as he quickly followed suit with his own plane. "The darker it gets, the better the chances of Nazi eyes not spotting us. Yeah, sure! But if that storm beats us to it, there'll be a ground wind that will knock *our* chances higher than a kite! And I don't mean maybe!"

That last most unpleasant consideration was uppermost in Dawson's brain as he and Freddy Farmer went tearing all out toward the southeast. And with every foot his Messerschmitt cut through the air, doubt and dread built itself up higher and higher within him. It was almost as though the gods of good fortune, and Lady Luck, had decided that they had done enough to help, and had quit cold on the job. Though Dawson's Messerschmitt was rocketing down across the shadowy sky, the storm clouds seemed to possess twice his speed. And with each rushing toward the other, the distance between them just shriveled away like snow in a blast furnace.

Eyes grim, and jaw set at a determined angle, Dawson hunched forward over the controls and searched the ground ahead and below. The bouncing lead came back to the pit of his stomach with a gleeful vengeance, for the ground was now almost lost in the swirling shadows of the approaching storm. It was almost impossible to pick out Tobolsk itself, to say nothing of the location of Nina's house in the Y of the two intersecting roads.

Suddenly, though, a voice seemed to cry out at him from nowhere; cry out to look down and to the left. Just exactly what urged him to do that, he didn't know. But he obeyed the sudden impulse, and his heart started pounding with wild hope again. Down there to the left he saw the Y formed by the two roads. He even saw Nina's house, if that pile of timber and stone could be called a house. And he was able to catch a fleeting glimpse of the small but apparently smooth field just to the left of the Y. Just a fleeting glimpse of the field before a moving sheet of rain cut across his vision. The advance guard of the storm had arrived. The race had turned out a tie, which to those two fighting eagles up in the air was just about the same as losing the race.

"But down we go!" Dawson roared out aloud. "Down we go, just the same. And, please, God, we've *got* to make it!"

As he gulped out the prayerful plea, he peered over at Freddy Farmer, who was still hugging close to his right wing tip, storm or no storm. At the same instant the English youth turned his own head Dawson's way, and then nodded it violently as though he had read the Yank's thoughts. Dave nodded back, lifted one hand in brief salute, then turned his face forward again, and gave every ounce of his undivided attention to his Messerschmitt.

An hour, a day, or it could have been a year passed before he had practically pushed the Messerschmitt down and around so that it was heading for the long way of the field, and into the snarling wind. He didn't know, and he didn't care, he was too busy working his throttle to maintain forward speed, and prevent the Messerschmitt from stalling. At times his forward speed matched the speed of the wind, and his plane almost stood still in the air just off the surface of the ground. And then suddenly his wheels touched. The plane bounced wildly, but he goosed the engine, and checked a disastrous second meeting with the wind-swept ground. When the wheels touched again, the Messerschmitt stayed down, and Dawson taxied it at a fast clip straight ahead and then off to the side to get out of the way of Freddy Farmer right behind him.

As a matter of fact, he had no sooner killed the engine, and leaped to the ground, while the Messerschmitt still trundled forward, than he saw the English youth's plane settle. Settle? It started to do just that, but a savage cross-wind caught it, and the aircraft came down like five tons of brick dumped off a high building. A wild cry of alarm rose up in Dawson's throat, but his zooming heart won the race to his mouth and choked it off. For a lifetime, it seemed, he could only stand rooted helplessly to the ground while Freddy Farmer's Messerschmitt jumped and leaped crazily about like a chip of wood on the crest of a raging sea. A dozen times the aircraft seemed to start over on its back, but somehow the English youth managed to keep it top side up. True, it skidded around in half-circles, first one way and then the other. But the wing tip didn't quite catch and grab on the ground to pile up the whole works in a heap. And then suddenly something seemed to shoot right out of the cockpit of the bouncing and dancing plane and down onto the ground.

Dawson blinked twice before he realized that that something was Freddy Farmer in the flesh, and that the English youth had raced over to where he stood, while the storm wind gleefully picked up the Messerschmitt and carried it the rest of the way down the field and smacked it up against some trees.

"Too bad, even if it is a Nazi plane!" Dawson heard Farmer's gasping voice. "But I couldn't nurse-maid the blasted thing forever. I had to let it go. Well, that must be the house, what?"

Dawson didn't bother to reply. Freddy had pulled another miracle out of the hat, and that part of the show was over. He just nodded quickly, then spun around on his heel, and went dashing over toward the lone house with Freddy Farmer at his heels. No lights were showing, but Dawson didn't even bother to knock. When he reached the front door he just grabbed hold of the knob, twisted it, shoved open the door and barged right inside. And both Freddy and he just managed to skid to a halt as they saw a small, thin figure come at them, and saw the glint of a gun barrel in the pale glow shed by a single lighted candle on a nearby table.

"Hey! Hold everything!" Dawson heard his own voice pant.

The last half of it, though, was drowned out by an even sharper cry in Russian. And before the echo was gone Senior Lieutenant Petrovski had appeared out of nowhere and leaped between Dawson and the advancing thin shadow. And a second or so later Dawson saw the tattered clothing, the wrinkled face, and the snow white hair of the thin "shadow." And then the Senior Lieutenant was talking to him.

"That was not wise, Captain!" she was saying sharply. "It is lucky I cried out in time, or Nina might have used that gun."

"Yeah, my error," Dawson grunted. "I was dumb. But in this storm I didn't figure that our knock would be heard. Besides, Farmer and I were in a hurry. Look, Senior Lieutenant! From here on we've got to stay in high gear. I mean, we've got to get going, and keep going. No telling when Lady Luck may quit on us. I don't think there's much of a guard on our bomber now. And this storm doesn't exactly hurt the situation, either. Where're Jones, and Nikolsk? The five of us have got to make tracks. You lead the way to the bomber, and we'll be right behind you with Nikolsk. I—Hey! The look on your face! Nikolsk isn't—he isn't—?"

"No, he is not dead, yet," the girl told him quickly. "He was even conscious for a little bit. And he did recognize Agent Jones. He even spoke of things a little. But not one millionth enough. And now he is unconscious again. I have great fear. He may never be conscious again. But what about the bomber? There is a chance to get him to a Moscow hospital?"

"What we're going to do!" Dawson told her firmly. "So let's do the talking later. Lead us to Nikolsk, and let's get going!"

The Russian girl didn't bother with any more words. She nodded for Dave and Freddy to follow, and led the way through a door to a rear room. The smell of Death itself seemed to hang in the air, and when Dawson glanced down at the thin, almost fleshless, and war-ravaged face of the figure wrapped tightly in blankets, his heart seemed to stop and turn into a chunk of ice. Ivan Nikolsk looked like a man who had died years before.

"Good grief, you two? Splendid! Thought all the racket was Gestapo lads breaking in. Now, what do we—?"

"We go!" Dawson broke into the middle of the question, and grinned into Agent Jones' strained and haggard face. "In the B-Twenty-Five, if luck is still pitching for our team. Never mind the questions, though. Save them until we get to Moscow. And we *will* get there! Okay, Senior Lieutenant! Please tell your Nina that we will never forget what she has done, and—But, hey! Do you think she'd like to try and make the trip with us?"

Before the girl Soviet Intelligence officer could speak, the small, thin, aged Russian woman appeared in the doorway.

"No, gallant ones," she said in halting English. "Here I have been, and here I stay. The Nazis do not bother with an old hag, as I am. So here I remain, and perhaps do more for my beloved Russia. No, go, gallant ones. And the arms of the Blessed Mother be about you!"

Dawson looked at her, and then, hardly realizing that he was doing so, he stepped quickly forward and took the old woman in his arms and kissed her reverently on the forehead. Then, face flaming red, he turned and went over to the bedside of Ivan Nikolsk.

"Put a part of the blanket over his face, Jones!" he said gruffly. "Blowing like blazes outside. And put your service automatic where you can grab it in a hurry. We may bump into trouble, and we may not. Okay! Take his legs, and I'll take his shoulders and head. Okay, Senior Lieutenant! This time we are going. And God love you, Nina!"

Dawson didn't realize he had flung the last at the aged Russian woman until he was outside in the cold driving rain and, with Agent Jones, was lugging the dying Nikolsk along in the wake of Freddy Farmer and the Russian girl. And when he did realize it he told himself that he had meant it with all his heart. Nina was but one of thousands of unknown heroes and heroines suffering under the steel heel of Hitlerism. No medals for those such as she. No statues, no anything. But God knew of each and every one of them, and the complete reward for their services to mankind would be theirs thricefold some day.

However, Dawson was actually only thinking those things in one tiny corner of his brain. The rest of his brain was busy with the task of ordering his legs and muscles to keep going, and keep close to Freddy Farmer and the Russian girl. But it was like stumbling through the very bottom of a long forgotten coal mine. Maybe Nasha Petrovski had the eyes of a cat, and so could see each tree trunk and ditch and stone that came up out of the rain slashed darkness. But Dawson didn't, and neither did Agent Jones. And so they stumbled and reeled and lurched forward, fighting every inch of the way to keep hold of their precious burden.

Twice during the long, long "years" that dragged by, Freddy Farmer dropped back and insisted on relieving either Dawson or Jones, but both of them refused the offer.

"Stick with her, Freddy!" Dave panted. "If there's trouble ahead, you two eagle eyes will spot it sooner. Thanks just the same, pal."

And so it continued on—forever and ever—and seemingly without end. A thousand times the cold fear that the Russian girl had lost her way clutched at Dawson's heart. As for himself, he had no idea where in the world they were. The black of night closed in from all sides. The wind-driven rain cut and slashed down into his face with the sting of white hot needle points. And the howl of the storm in his ears was like some invisible force trying to pry off the top of his head. He wanted to cry out to the others to stop and rest a moment, but the words just wouldn't come. And each time he felt that urge he was both relieved and ashamed when it was gone.

And then suddenly the little party groping cross-country through the black, stormy night did come to a halt. It was the Russian girl who brought them to a halt. And her voice came to them through the howl of the storm almost like a whisper.

"The edge of the woods is but a step ahead!" she said. "Beyond it, the bomber. I do not think there are many guards, but there must be some. This, then, is a task for me. Remain motionless, please. But when you hear three quick shots from my revolver, come as though the entire German army were right behind you. It will not be long. This is what I do gladly for my Russia."

A sharp bark of protest came up into Dawson's mouth, but there it died in silence, for the spot of rain-swept darkness that had held the Russian girl was only a spot of rain-swept darkness now. She had gone in a flash, and the three youths could only hold up Ivan Nikolsk as gently as they could—and wait—each with his own thoughts.

However, there didn't seem to be any waiting period at all—at least not over thirty seconds at the most. Suddenly, from out of the wind-howling darkness ahead, came three distinct shots from a revolver! Nobody said anything. Nobody so much as let out a shout of joy. Dawson, Agent Jones, and Freddy Farmer simply hoisted Ivan Nikolsk up to a more comfortable position, and went plunging forward through the black stormy night. And in practically no time at all there was level ground under their feet, and they were running over toward the darker blur that was the B-Twenty-Five bomber.

"Here, to your left!" the voice of Senior Lieutenant Petrovski suddenly spoke in Dawson's ear. "Here is the bomber door. And watch out for those dead ones on the ground. There were five, and as I suspected they were inside the bomber to be out of the storm. They were surprised, and then they were dead. But here—give me your place. You must get in and start the engines. The three of us will manage. And may it be His wish that Ivan Nikolsk still lives!"

"And keeps living. Amen!" Dawson echoed as he shifted his share of the burden to the Russian girl's strong arms. "But how in the world did you—?"

"A knife makes no noise!" she cut him off almost harshly. "And the knives of Russia are very sharp!"

That's all Dawson wanted to know. He leaped past the girl, stumbled over the feet of some dead Nazi guard, and then ducked through the bomber's door, and made his way forward to the pilots' compartment. It seemed that he had hardly dropped into the seat, and was shooting out his hand for the switches, when Freddy Farmer dropped into the co-pilot's seat alongside.

"The chap's regaining consciousness again, Dave!" the English youth cried wildly. "Agent Jones is back there with him, with his notebook. Get us off, old thing, in a hurry. Blast if we're not going to grab this one out of thin air, too. What a girl, that Senior Lieutenant!"

"You mean, what an army!" Dawson shouted at him as he jabbed the starter buttons. "She's a whole doggone army, all by herself. And, boy, can she think way out in front of a guy, too! She's—"

The most welcome sound in all the world drowned out Dawson's voice at that moment: the powerful, thunderous roar of the B-Twenty-Five's twin Wright Cyclones coming to life. For a few precious seconds Dawson let them roar so that they would warm up as fast as possible. But at the end of that time he saw spitting flame off to the left and ahead, and the left side window of the pilots' compartment seemed to blow in on him in a shower of splintered glass.

"Get going, Dave!" Freddy Farmer cried excitedly.

"Get, nothing!" Dawson roared back. "We're *gone!*"

And even as the first word spilled off his lips he had kicked off the wheel brakes, forked the throttles wide open and was booting the B-Twenty-Five around the necessary half-turn to get it headed toward the far end of the field. And then as the bomber went forward, picking up speed with every powerful revolution of its propellers, orange, red, and yellow flame sparked and stabbed the darkness on both sides. Dawson felt bullets smash into the bomber, and even heard some of them twang off the engine cowlings, but the twin Cyclones did not miss a single beat, and the B-Twenty-Five went thundering forward until the wings could get their teeth in the air, and Dawson was able to lift the ship clear and nose it upward into the stormy night.

When no more than a couple of thousand feet were under his wings, he leveled off, checked with the automatic compass, and then swung the B-Twenty-Five around toward the north.

"Back to your job of navigating, Freddy, old sock!" he shouted at his pal. "Moscow next stop, and we're in a hurry. So you see to it that we hit it on the nose, hey, kid?"

"Have I ever missed?" Freddy snapped at him.

"Well, anyway," Dawson grinned back at him, "see that you don't make *this* the first time!"

Clear, brilliant sunshine flooded the length and breadth of Moscow. Four wonderful days Dawson, Agent Jones, and Freddy Farmer had spent in the fascinating Soviet city. Four swell days of sight-seeing, and banquets for heroes—themselves. Though the three of them had insisted that the major share of the glory belonged to Senior Lieutenant Petrovski, who had as quickly disappeared out of their lives as she had come into them.

As a matter of fact, five minutes after Dawson had landed the B-Twenty-Five on the Moscow military airport, the pretty-looking Russian girl was gone, just like that. And Colonel General Vladimir, who was at the airport to greet them, had explained in a few words, with a meaningful smile.

"When the war is won, her work will be done," he said. "But the war is not won, yet. And there are still many things to be done."

And so, just like that, the pretty Russian girl had stepped right out of their lives, and they had been more or less forced to accept her share of the glory. But it was not so much the glory as it was the unspoken prayers of thankfulness in their hearts that really blotted black memories from their minds, and let them enjoy their short stay in Moscow. A thankfulness that God had not let Ivan Nikolsk die, but had shielded his frail body from that final blast of Nazi death as Dawson had taken that bomber off the Tobolsk field. Shielded Nikolsk's body. And done even more. Had let him live so that he reached the Moscow hospital. And given him the strength to tell all of his share of the secret to Agent Jones, *and* to no less than Premier Joseph Stalin himself!

Neither Dawson nor Freddy Farmer had been present. Their part of the job had been done. Besides, they had no real desire to hear a ghost of a man gasp out words that must first be fitted in with other words already known to United Nations Intelligence to make any sense. But later, when Agent Jones had joined them at their suite in the International Hotel, one look at his face had told them that more than a battlefield victory had been won. Important, invaluable information about enemy intentions had been gained. And in war, knowledge of what the enemy plans to do is a victory already won. So they had been content to keep questions off their tongues. Besides, Agent Jones' final job was to make his secret report to his superior, Air Vice-Marshal Leman, and to no one else.

However, as the three youths sat lounging about in their suite, resting before the final banquet in their honor—for they would leave for England on the morrow—Dawson stared hard at Agent Jones' good-looking face for a long minute, and could no longer hold back the question that had been in his mind ever since that luncheon in Simpson's.

"Your name isn't Jones, but Leman—right?" he practically blurted out.

Agent Jones stiffened and gave him a startled look. Then he grinned slowly, and sighed.

"A chap can't keep a thing from you, can he?" he said.

"Not when he's got a face as good-looking as his Dad's, who's an Air Vice-Marshal," Dave replied with a chuckle. "And, boy, *I* was the guy who told your Dad that you were probably imagining things, such as being followed, and your room searched, and stuff! No wonder he practically blew me down with a look!"

"Oh, so that's why you asked me if something about this chap didn't strike me, eh?" Freddy Farmer spoke up. "Good gosh! I thought you knew that for certain. Why, it was obvious, old thing. Anybody—"

"Come off it, pal!" Dawson cried threateningly, and picked up a book. "Don't give me that. *You* didn't even guess, until Jones admitted it just now."

Freddy Farmer made a face, and walked over to the door.

"Rubbish!" he snorted. "We English chaps just keep things like that to ourselves. Not nosy, like *some* chaps I know. Well, I'll leave you two for a spell. A bit of shopping I must do. But I say, Jones—I mean, Leman—?"

Freddy opened the door, half turned, and grinned wickedly.

"I leave you, Leman, old thing, in honored company, you know," he chuckled. "Oh, quite! *A gallant soldier all Russia must admire!*"

And then Freddy Farmer leaped out into the hall as the book Dawson had been holding smacked against the inside of the door where Freddy Farmer's head had been just a moment before!

THE END

Page from

DAVE DAWSON
WITH THE FLYING TIGERS

ISBN: 1519556772

The music was soft and soothing; like no other music ever heard on earth before. And all about was beauty far beyond the power of words to depict, or the brush of an artist. Everything was so wonderful, so perfect, and so—

But through Dawson's throbbing, pounding head slipped a tiny inkling of the stark, naked truth. There was no soft, soothing music, there was no breath-taking beauty, and nothing was wonderful, or even approaching perfection. All was Death. Horrible, lingering, painful death that comes to a man lost, and unarmed, in the steaming lush jungle of north Burma.

Yes, it was just his brain, and all of his senses playing him tricks originated by the Devil. Tricks to make him let go, and just relax—and die. But he wouldn't let go. He wouldn't die. He couldn't. There was too much to—

The whine of engines pulled his head up out of the mud and slime. He rolled half over, gritted his teeth against the pain, and peered up through the twisted canopy of jungle growth.

EASTERN FRONT MAPS, 1943,1944

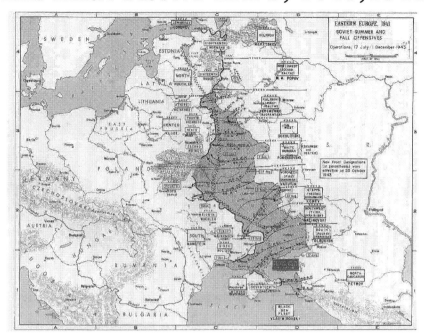

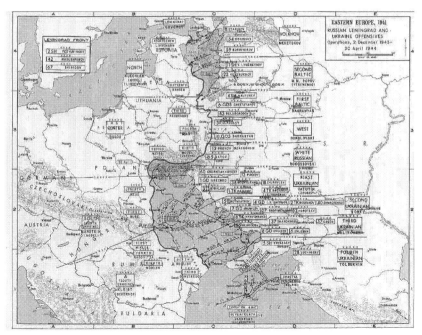

DAVE DAWSON

ISBN 1523604409

ISBN 1523604255

ISBN 1523604352

ISBN 1523604387

DAVE DAWSON

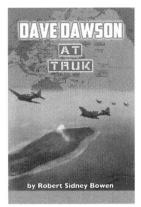

ISBN 1519556543

ISBN 1519556500

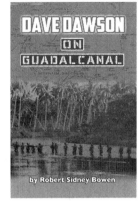

ISBN 1519556799

ISBN 1519556934

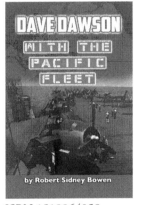

ISBN 1518864058

ISBN 1519556772

ISBN 1519556721

ISBN 1519556632

ISBN 1519556942

www.alacritypress.com

G.A. Henty Books by Alacrity Press

Captain Bayley's Heir
A Tale of the Gold Fields of California
by G.A. HENTY

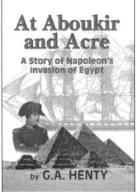

At Aboukir and Acre
A Story of Napoleon's Invasion of Egypt
by G.A. HENTY

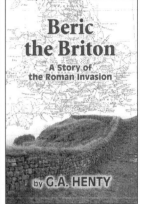

Beric the Briton
A Story of the Roman Invasion
by G.A. HENTY

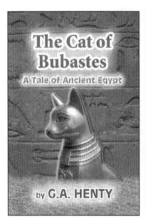

The Cat of Bubastes
A Tale of Ancient Egypt
by G.A. HENTY

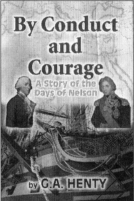

By Conduct and Courage
A Story of the Days of Nelson
by G.A. HENTY

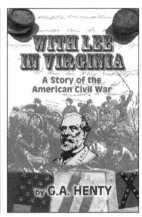

WITH LEE IN VIRGINIA
A Story of the American Civil War
by G.A. HENTY

Two Books in One
With Moore at Corunna
&
Under Wellington's Command
Tales of the Peninsular War
by G.A. HENTY

Maori and Settler
A Story of the New Zealand War
by G.A. HENTY

For the Temple
A Tale of the Fall of Jerusalem
by G.A. HENTY

WORLD WAR II COMES ALIVE!

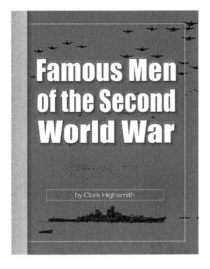

World War II was the most complex event in history, the consequences of which are still being felt today. Believing that one of the best ways to learn history is through biography, **Famous Men of the Second World War** tells the story of the war through the lives of thirty-one men (and women!). **Famous Men of the Second World War** investigates the lives of prominent men, including George Patton and Winston Churchill, as well as lesser-known men, including Carl Mannerheim and Chiang Kai-shek.

Famous Men of the Second World War attempts to shed light on topics often overlooked in World War II texts, examining the important role of China, Russia's 1939 Winter War with Finland, the rescue of thousands of Hungarian Jews from the Holocaust and the epic clash between Germany and Russian on the Eastern Front.

Review questions are included for each chapter to supplement home or classroom study.

Available from Alacrity Press.

Visit the book website at:
wwww.famousmenww2.com

Made in the USA
Middletown, DE
23 December 2022

20304651R00078